# Emily and the DEVIL

By Jasminne A. McDonald

# "Warning!"

*"This book is for adult readers only. It contains mature content and language that may not be suitable for children."*

# Table of Contents

# Acknowledgement

I want to thank three people who played a special role in encouraging me on this journey.

First, my job coach, Ms. Trula Freeman. I shared my manuscript with her, and not only did she enjoy it, but she also helped me shape the story so that it flowed more naturally and realistically. Her support meant a great deal.

Second, I want to thank Tamara Taylor, a kind woman I met at the airport who works for American Airlines. I showed her my book, and her interest and encouragement gave me an unexpected boost of confidence when I needed it most.

Third and finally, I would like to thank Andrea Hayes, another woman I met at the airport. I showed her my book, and she gave me the inspiration I needed to improve the story.

To three of you, thank you.

# Chapter 1

A young woman named Emily Richards lived in Halo Town, a small town. She lived with her family in a small house in the neighborhood. She was a person who struggled with her non-existence daily.

Although she was only 19 years old, she was treated like an outcast and consistently ignored by everyone who passed by her. But they only stopped doing things to hurt her feelings. Nobody paid her any attention. No guy would go out with her on a date. They only preferred pretty girls with fancy clothes and lots of money, something Emily didn't have. No one wanted to be her friend because they only made fun of her. From her face to the clothes she wore daily, she was odd, and people found her weird. She wore old, ragged, hand-me-down garments that didn't accentuate her womanly appearance. While other people wore clean, new, fancy clothes, Emily looked more like a dirty rag doll forgotten in a bargain bin at a discount toy store. Although intelligent, she was often called a nerd by her peers and the people in her town.

Since her childhood, Emily had always been unnoticed by everyone. Especially since she was the oddball who was always left out, they only focused on their oldest son, Marcus. However, they never showed her support or accepted her. She was nothing like her brother. He was more of an athlete, while Emily was the small, intelligent girl with no significant relationships. They kept her from going out after sundown each night, never letting her watch television or go shopping. They even disapproved of her dreams and wishes, which made her feel pathetic and miserable. She wished she were rich and pretty like the other girls and had a handsome man to date. Sadly, it never happened. Her parents intended for her to be grateful for her life and not rely on other people's lifestyles for her own. But nothing would make Emily happy.

Now, she was a first-year student at Halo University, a prestigious college located in Halo Town, where Emily's parents enrolled her. She took courses regularly, but she still struggled with her miserable life, which was hard for her.

The professors on campus never noticed her. All the students on campus would call her names and insult her when she wasn't looking. The students made it even more challenging for Emily because she was different from all the others on campus. The other students got to live in dormitory houses, but Emily still lived with her parents because they couldn't afford a dormitory room for her. No Sorority or Fraternity house would accept her.

Every day was the same for Emily, and there were no changes. She had no one to talk to, no friends to call, no boyfriend to date. She felt as if the world was against her for being here. She felt like a failure to everyone. Her life was empty whenever she wanted something, just like everybody else. But her wishes never came true. Until one day, her life was going to change forever.

It was a clear Tuesday morning in April. Emily was running late for college. She scrambled out of bed to get dressed quickly. Emily wore a pale blue wool sweater with faded, navy blue jeans. She fixed her tangled blonde hair and tried to put on her old, dirty, gray sneakers.

Emily ran downstairs and grabbed her bag in the living room. She didn't even say goodbye to her parents or stop for breakfast. Emily was in a hurry. She headed out the door of her house on her way to the University. However, she encountered many obstacles, which slowed her down on the way. A neighborhood dog chased her down the street. A group of boys threw mud at her. And she almost got run over by an oncoming Ford Mustang. She was also yelled at by an angry driver, who told her to watch where she was going. But she didn't have time to tell him she was sorry. She was already going to miss the first bell. Luckily, she managed to get to Halo University. By the time she arrived, she had made her way inside unseen.

She headed down the hallway and tried to reach her class before the bell rang. But as she did, she tripped on a wet floor sign.

**"OOF!"**

Emily looked up and found herself on the floor, being laughed at by her peers.

"Look where you're going next time," one of the students said. Three college students then arrived. Their names were Nicole, Jetta, and Katie. They were known as the popular girls of Halo University. They were rich, popular, and glamorous on and off campus. They wore expensive and fabulous fashion attire to impress their peers.

But they were also mean girls, especially toward Emily. Since she first enrolled here at Halo University as a first-year student, they mocked her by calling her names and making fun of her clothes. It hurt Emily's feelings. She didn't like being picked on by three of the most popular girls on campus. When they saw Emily on the floor, they made fun of her publicly.

"Look at the loser," said Nicole.

Jetta and Katie laughed with her in response.

"What a clumsy fool," said Jetta.

"You belong in a circus," said Katie. Emily felt ashamed of her humiliation. She got up off the floor and tried to confront them.

"I think you're a bunch of... a bunch of...," she tried her best, but didn't have anything to say in response to the three college girls.

They laughed at her again.

"You don't have shit to say," said Nicole. "You're pathetic. You don't belong here. Go home."

Nicole, Jetta, and Katie walked away while the rest of the college students went to class. Emily was left alone in the hallway. When the bell rang, she quickly headed to class.

When she arrived, she took her seat near the window in the classroom. Nobody seemed to notice her when she came in. The three identical girls came in as Emily tried to write down the assignment from the blackboard in her notebook.

Emily and The Devil

The other students gave them attention and appreciation, making Emily jealous and hurt. Professor Phillips, the English professor, entered the room and called the students to pay attention.

"Good morning, class," she said.

"Good morning, Professor Phillips," the students responded. Then, she gave them a test to take. However, when Professor Phillips approached Emily, she gave her a distasteful expression.

"Miss Richards," she said. "You will stay here after class to retake the test you failed."

Emily gasped, and the other students laughed at her. Especially the three girls.

"You should send her back to Kindergarten, Professor Phillips," said Nicole from a distance.

"That's quite enough, Miss Nicole," Professor Phillips said. She told the other students to be quiet. Then, Emily asked why she must retake her test. Professor Phillips explained that she received a grade of 32%, which was equivalent to an F. "I expect you to study more," Professor Phillips said. She returned to the blackboard and resumed writing down the remaining English quotes. When class ended, the students, except Emily, began to leave the classroom. She had to stay behind to retake her test.

Later that afternoon, Emily left the University, feeling sad and lonely. She was embarrassed about her mistake earlier. The students started teasing and laughing at her as she walked by, which made her feel ashamed.

"You suck, Richards," said a football player on campus.

"Go back to Preschool," said a cheerleader.

The rest of the students laughed.

Emily was pelted with insults by the students on campus, like arrows piercing her from behind. Just then, Nicole, Jetta, and Katie approached her.

"Look at the ugly duckling," said Jetta.

"That sweater looks so ugly," said Nicole. "Especially on someone as ugly as her!"

Tears began to form in Emily's eyes.

"Did your Mother dress you this morning?" said Nicole.

Jetta and Katie laughed. But Emily frowned because the three college girls hurt her feelings. "Leave me alone," she said.

"Whatever, geek," said Nicole bitterly. The girls walked off, snubbing her.

As the students began to leave, Emily walked down the street alone. She felt unconfident and unappreciated. She watched couples passing by holding hands and smiling at each other. But then, they looked at Emily and frowned.

"What a pathetic loser," said an elderly woman walking with her husband. Emily lowered her head. A few minutes later, Emily arrived in town. But as she walked, cars passed, splashing water and mud on her.

**"SPLASH!"**

Poor Emily was dirty, muddy, and wet all over. She was disappointed with her appearance. Her mother gave her the sweater, and now Emily had ruined it.

"What will my mother say when she sees this?" she said.

Emily headed into a small coffee shop near the bookstore. As she did, she found a table near the window. Emily sat down and sighed. She placed her hands on the table and looked at the menu. But Emily wasn't hungry. She didn't have any money with her.

Emily hung her head in sadness at the sight of her muddy sweater and messy hair reflected in the silver napkin holder on the table. Knowing how awful she looked, she didn't want to see herself in it. Then, she turned and looked at a window display of a fashion department store across the street. In the window was a fancy, floor-length, strapless, and shimmering red evening gown made of sequins in red and silver. She daydreamed about wearing that red evening dress and attending a beautiful ball like in the fairy tale books she once read as a child. All the guests would turn to look at her and admire her beauty. She also saw a handsome Prince dressed in white, dancing with her under the stars and moon.

Emily and The Devil

Emily sighed at the thought of being swept off her feet by a dreamy, handsome man. She imagined dancing under the starry sky in the arms of her Prince Charming and sharing a passionate kiss beneath the moon. Just then, a man approached Emily.

"Excuse me," he said.

Emily turned around and looked at the man standing next to her. She cleared her throat nervously.

"Oh, um, hello," she said.

The man looking at her was the coffee shop clerk. He looked at her oddly and frowned. "Are you gonna order something, or do I have to ask you to leave?" he asked.

Emily was disappointed. "No, I'll just leave," she said, her voice filled with sadness.

 Emily got up from her table and left the coffee shop. With a heavy heart, she began to make her way home. However, as Emily walked down the street, she looked at the window display again and started daydreaming. She imagined what it would be like to wear that dress for herself. But she knew it would never happen because her parents could never afford it for her.

A store clerk in the window removed the dress from the display and closed the curtains with a sign that read, "No clothes for poor people."

Emily's eyes filled with tears as she watched the townspeople wearing fancy attire and walking down the street to attend fancy events and exquisite banquets. She felt like a poor, hungry, and penniless peasant.

"I'd give anything to have a luxurious lifestyle," she said to herself.

She turned away from the window display and walked off down the sidewalk. Suddenly, she bumped into a man on the same sidewalk.

**"OOF!"**

Emily tried to apologize for bumping into him. But as she was about to, she looked up at him and gazed into his eyes. He was a tall, handsome man. He stood 6 feet tall with broad shoulders, a muscular chest, and long legs. He wore a red suit with a black tie. He looked like a businessman or a male model. He had slick, black hair, dark brown eyes, and a chiseled face like Adonis's. He was gorgeous.

The man looked at her with a seductive stare. "Hello," he said in a low, velvet voice. "I usually don't bump into people, but you're the first to bump into me."

Emily got lost in his dreamy gaze. She could feel her heart beating in her chest. "*ba-dum—ba-dum—ba-dum.*" The sound echoed in her ears. Her face turned crimson with embarrassment. She had never seen a man stare at her before. She hid her face and quickly backed away.

"Excuse me," she said. "I have to go."

Without looking back, Emily ran all the way home. The mysterious man was left standing in confusion.

As Emily came home, she headed inside and closed the door. Her heart was still racing, and her face remained flushed. Just then, her mother came in.

Emily shrieked.

Mrs. Richards, Emily's mother, asked what was wrong with her.

"Nothing," said Emily nervously. She quickly ran upstairs to her bedroom to hide. Her mother was left confused. "There's something wrong with her," she thought.

In her bedroom, Emily hid her face in the pillow. She couldn't stop thinking about the tall, handsome man she bumped into. She thought he would be mad at her for ruining his suit with her muddy sweater. But just the sight of his face left her feeling flushed. The image burned within her mind. His face and his eyes were the only things she could see.

As she tried to calm down, there was a knock on the door. Emily sat up in her bed and tried to collect herself. "Come in," she said. The door opened, and in stood her mother. She wore a cotton apron with flower patterns and yellow oven mitts on her hands.

"Is there something you want to tell me?" she asked. Emily didn't answer. She was still embarrassed. Her mother frowned.

"Emily Richards," she said. "I want an answer." So Emily got up from her bed to tell her. But as she was about to say a word, her mother looked at her muddy sweater. "What have you done to your sweater?" her mother said.

Emily sighed and lowered her head. "I got splashed with mud," she said. Her mother was disappointed to see her daughter covered in mud.

"Go change for dinner," she said strictly.

Emily left her bedroom and returned to the kitchen, where her mother cooked dinner for the family that night. Emily lay back down on her bed and closed her eyes for a brief moment. But as she did, the same image of the man she had bumped into reappeared.

That evening, Emily came downstairs to join her family for dinner. Her brother, Marcus, entered the room, wearing a basketball jersey and athletic sneakers. As Emily washed her hands, she turned to look at Marcus, who was getting a glass of milk from the refrigerator.

"What's the matter, Emily?" he said. "Forget your bib and highchair?"

Emily frowned at Marcus. "I'm not a baby," she told him. Marcus came up to Emily and pinched her cheek.

"Someone needs her bottle," he said with a laugh. Emily didn't like how her brother was treating her. Then, Mrs. Richards called everyone to the table. Marcus was the first to reach the table because he was taller and faster than Emily.

Marcus sat down at the table while Emily was the last to take a seat. But when she came to the table, her parents gave her a plate of white bread and spinach.

"What is this?" she said, making a face of disgust.

Mr. Richards frowned at Emily. "Don't make faces and eat your dinner," he said.

Emily didn't like what was on her plate. "It looks more like slime on a tombstone to me," she said. She preferred to eat something other than spinach and bread. She wanted to avoid the food that was on her plate.

Mrs. Richards looked at Emily. "Eat your spinach and bread, Emily," she said. "Don't just sit there looking at it. You need your vitamins."

Emily groaned. She didn't want to eat spinach and bread for dinner. "Why can't I eat something nice and colorful?" she asked.

Her parents said nothing. While she was left eating a plate of spinach and bread, Marcus had a healthy, delicious dinner—a plate of meatloaf, mixed vegetables, baked potatoes, and spaghetti with meatballs.

Emily watched as Marcus told her parents how he won the basketball game. "Ten seconds on the clock," he said. "I was going to make the shot before the buzzer struck." Mr. and Mrs. Richards listened as Marcus told them about the basketball game.

Emily felt left out by her own family. They seemed to care more about Marcus than they did about her. They hardly knew she was there at the table with a plate of spinach and bread. Marcus continued telling his family about the game. "Greg passes the ball to Michael," he said. "Five seconds left. Michael passes it to me. I shot the ball into the hoop, and the time was up. We won the game."

Mr. and Mrs. Richards were happy that Marcus had won the game. They felt proud.

"Congratulations, son," said Mr. Richards.

"You get a special reward tonight," said Mrs. Richards.

"Chocolate ice cream and cake for dessert." Marcus smiled at receiving dessert for winning the basketball game. However, Emily was feeling upset and jealous at the same time. Being ignored by her parents at the dinner table was too much for her to bear.

"I can't take it anymore," she yelled. "I'm going to bed now." So she excused herself from the table to go to bed. She didn't want to hear more of her brother's stories about his games. As she went upstairs to her room, she removed her dirty hand-me-down clothes and put them in the hamper.

Emily was tired of her non-existence. She was upset about wearing poor hand-me-down clothes and being fed white bread and spinach for dinner. She was tired of her unfulfilling, mundane life and feeling unnoticed. She was tired of the plain, boring pajamas she slept in every night. She wished she had a life of luxury. She wanted to wake up in a bed of silk and satin sheets rather than plain, gray cotton ones. She also wanted breakfast to be served to her in bed, like a princess. She wished for a breakfast tray instead of a bowl of cold oatmeal. On her tray would be a breakfast made just for her. She wanted a glass of orange juice, a plate of sausage, scrambled eggs, hash browns drizzled with ranch dressing, and French toast with syrup and powdered sugar.

Emily even wanted to be dressed in fancy, lavish clothes that made her look like a movie star or a celebrity, and to arrive at Halo University in style—a long stretch limousine with a private flat-screen TV in the back seat for her to watch. And at dinner, she wanted to dine at a fancy restaurant, wearing a red evening gown. She could see herself sitting at a table reserved just for her, surrounded by the glow of candlelight. Emily sighed at the thought of having a life like that. So, she wished to lead a life of luxury. Then, Emily turned out the light and went to bed. As she slept, she began to dream of having a luxurious lifestyle.

# Chapter 2

The next day, Emily took ballet lessons in Ms. Welch's ballet class. The other college girls were practicing with her while Ms. Welch was instructing them. They were rehearsing for the Halo University production of the ballet, "Swan Lake." Emily was playing one of the swans in the show. She had been dancing ballet since she was 5 years old. However, the other dancers didn't like her. They thought she was clumsy with her dancing. They would call her names such as "Clumsy Duck."

While reviewing the dance choreography, Emily still yearned for a luxurious lifestyle. But simultaneously, she was still thinking of the man she had seen the day before. The look in his eyes captivated her. He drew her close to him like a magnet. She felt his gaze hypnotize her, and seeing how he looked at her made her heart beat again. She felt a little feverish. She almost fainted. Nevertheless, it distracted her from her practice, and she was unable to focus.

Ms. Welch, the ballet instructor, clapped her hands loudly in front of Emily.

"Ms. Richards," she yelled. "Pay attention! Honestly, where is your head today?"

Emily looked at Ms. Welch and got nervous. "I'm sorry," she said. "I guess I was distracted."

Ms. Welch approached her and grabbed her arm in a firm grip. "This is supposed to be a ballet!" she said in a strict voice. "You are a swan, and swans don't drift off and dream. They dance! Now quit your daydreaming and get back to work!"

Emily apologized for her lack of focus and promised to try again. However, Nicole then began to make fun of her. "Maybe she should play the ugly duckling instead," she said.

All the other college girls started to laugh. But Ms. Welch told them all to be quiet. "Let's not call people names," she said. "Please resume your positions." Then, she pointed at Emily with a frown. "And you, Ms. Richards," she said. "No mistakes." Emily swallowed nervously. The others snickered behind her.

So, all the girls returned to their ballet positions to resume the dance. Emily, however, tried her best to stay focused. But try as she did, it only made it worse. The image of the tall, handsome man reappeared in her head as Emily tried to dance. But now she pictured him dancing with her in the mirror. His arm wrapped around her waist while his left hand slowly stroked down her body in a sensual manner. She felt a chill down her spine, imagining his mouth on her skin and leaving a trail of kisses down her neck and onto her shoulder. Emily turned to face him. But as she did, she tripped on her ballet slipper and fell to the floor.

**"BOOM!"**

Ms. Welch stopped the music and called out to Emily. "Miss Richard," she yelled. "I warned you."

The college girls laughed at Emily because of the way she was dancing and how she fell to the floor.

"Look at the clumsy duck," said Jetta.

"She has two left feet," said Katie.

Everyone began to chant and point at Emily. "Clumsy duck, clumsy duck. Emily's a clumsy duck." Emily covered her ears to block out the name-calling. It was hurting her feelings. Ms. Welch was angry at her for ruining the choreography.

"I'm afraid I'll have to dismiss you from ballet class," she said.

Emily was saddened to leave ballet class because of her clumsiness and lack of focus. She got up off the floor and began to leave. But then, Nicole stuck out her foot and made Emily trip.

Everyone laughed again.

Emily started to cry. She left the room for the remainder of the day while the rest of the girls resumed dancing. As she changed out of her ballet leotard, she put on her old hand-me-down clothes in the locker room. Still sad, Emily went down the hall to her next class.

Later that day, Emily was taking a test in Professor Phillips' English class. But she was having trouble staying focused because she was still thinking about the tall, handsome man. Her heart was pounding inside her chest like a jackhammer. Her breath shortened and quickened as if she were in a state of panic. Then, Professor Phillips approached her and slammed a ruler hard on Emily's desk.

**"SMACK!!"** It startled Emily.

She looked at the Professor in fear. She looked angry. "Ms. Richards," Professor Phillips said. "Do I have to send you to the Dean's office?"

Emily shook her head. "No, Ma'am," she said. However, Professor Phillips noticed that Emily's face was turning red.

"Are you feeling okay?" she asked. "Do you need to see a doctor?"

Emily shook her head again, trying to hide her embarrassment. "I'm fine," said Emily. Professor Phillips thought she might be having a fever, but she disapproved. She told Emily to stay after class to finish her test. Emily lowered her head in humiliation, too distracted by thoughts of the mysterious man.

Throughout the day, Emily sadly walked down the hallway, trying to banish the image of the man from her mind. But the harder she tried, the more distracted she became. Emily bumped into other students who told her to stay out of the way. As she passed by a mirror in the hallway, she could see herself in the arms of the mysterious, handsome man from this morning. She could see that he was about to kiss her on the lips as he held her in his arms. The seductive look in his eyes was piercing her soul in the mirror, as if she were under his spell, and she couldn't break free.

Emily slowly tried to back away, but accidentally bumped into the lockers before falling onto the floor again. It broke her from her hypnotic trance for now. She quickly got up and ran down the hallway to her next class.

Later that afternoon, Emily arrived home. She had some homework to do in her backpack. As Emily entered the house, her parents were in the living room. They called out to Emily as she made her way inside.

"Hi, Mom and Dad," she said shyly. Her parents were angry at her. They told her they had received a call from Professor Phillips at Halo University.

"You've been daydreaming in class again," Mr. Richards said.

Emily trembled. "I can explain," she said. But Mr. Richards told her to be quiet. He didn't want to hear her explanation about her daydreaming in college.

"Your Professor says you have been falling behind on your grades," he said. "How do you expect to graduate from college?"

Emily shook her head in disagreement with her Father's words. "I promise it won't happen again," she said. But her parents didn't believe her. It made Emily grow angry. So she went upstairs to her room to do her homework.

Then, Marcus emerged from his bedroom wearing a fresh, clean basketball jersey and athletic sneakers. He noticed Emily and approached her.

"What huge mistake did Mom and Dad send you up to your room for this time?" he asked.

Emily told him her parents are mad at her for falling behind in her grades at college. "I was daydreaming in class," she said.

Marcus laughed. "Poor, stupid Emily failed yet again," he said. "I wish I had a smarter sister."

Emily frowned. "Don't call me names," she said. "I'm still your sister."

But Marcus didn't care. He stuck his tongue out at her before heading downstairs. He was going to the gym to train for his upcoming basketball game.

Emily watched as her parents wished him luck. "Be back in time for supper," Mrs. Richards said.

"Thanks, Mom," Marcus said.

Emily was distraught. Marcus was the only one getting the attention from her parents, but not from her. It made Emily furious.

"I can't believe you guys," she said. "Why does he get all the good treatment but not me?"

Mr. Richards gave Emily a disappointing look, and Emily went to her room in frustration. She closed the door with a loud

**"SLAM!"**

In her room, Emily tried to do her homework, but as she attempted to focus, she found herself imagining the mysterious man again. Emily couldn't stop thinking about it. She suddenly started drawing pictures of him in her notebook. His face bore a dark, seductive stare, a gorgeous smile, and a handsome physique, all accentuated by a red suit. Emily blushed hard at seeing what she had drawn in her notebook. However, she snapped herself out of it and tried to control her emotions, as she still had to complete her homework. So she said to herself, "Focus, Emily." Over and over, she repeated those words to stay focused on her studies, undistracted.

Unfortunately, the same image of the mysterious man kept appearing in her mind. Almost as if he were luring her away from the task at hand. She couldn't get the image out of her head.

Over the next few days, Emily attempted to clear the image of the man from her mind by focusing on something else. But no matter what she did, she could still picture the man. During class and at home, Emily continued to think of the tall, handsome man and heard his low, velvet voice in her ears. He seemed to be attracted to her when he saw her.

The students began to tease her for daydreaming. They thought she was crazy, but she wasn't. Emily was feeling even more embarrassed. The thought of seeing the mysterious man she had bumped into was making Emily lose her concentration in her courses. It even upset her parents about her poor performance in her classes.

One month later, Emily was leaving Halo University after another awful day in May. She grew increasingly frustrated with the humiliating moments she was experiencing on campus. She needed to get her mind off the mysterious man before something went wrong. So, she returned to the coffee shop downtown to clear her mind. But when she arrived, to her surprise, there was the same tall, handsome man she had bumped into about a month ago. He was sitting by the window, drinking a cup of coffee. Emily's face turned red, and her heart beat louder. She couldn't breathe. She attempted to leave without being seen. But as she did, she accidentally bumped into a counter and knocked over a display of coffee mugs.

**"CRASH!!"**

The loud sound caught everyone's attention. Emily fell to the floor along with the shattered coffee mugs.

The coffee clerk came out here to see what was going on. When he saw Emily on the floor, he got angry. "Look at this mess," he roared. "You'll have to pay for these mugs."

Emily felt ashamed of her clumsiness. She tried to clean up the mess, but kept knocking over things from the counter. It made the clerk even angrier. "You break it, you buy it," he said.

"But I don't have any money," Emily cried.

The handsome man noticed Emily and remembered her bumping into him. A seductive grin appeared on his face. He got up from his table and walked over to Emily.

"Need any help?" he asked.

Emily looked up at the tall, handsome man. Their eyes met just like before. Her cheeks were crimson at the sight of his face. The clerk told him to leave because Emily had to pay for the shattered coffee mugs she had knocked over. But he raised his hand in protest.

"I'll pay for the damage," the handsome man said. He took out a maroon-colored wallet and pulled out eighty-five dollars. He paid for the shattered coffee mugs and helped Emily clean up the mess.

After he cleaned up the mess, the handsome man helped Emily onto her feet. "Thank you for saving my life," said Emily with relief.

The man smiled. "My pleasure," he said. "It's the least I can do for a Damsel in distress." He took Emily's hand and kissed it gently. Emily pulled her hand away and wiped it on her faded jeans.

"Who are you?" she asked.

The man straightened his tie and began to introduce himself to her. "My name is Mr. Lucien Redd," he said. "I am the CEO of Redd Enterprises in Diablo City. But you can call me Mr. Redd. What's your name?"

Emily cleared her throat. "I'm Emily Richards," she replied.

Mr. Redd looked at Emily with a seductive look in his eyes. "You're beautiful," he said. "I remember you bumping into me a month ago. I said you were the first to bump into me."

Hearing those words, Emily remembered her embarrassing encounter with him while walking home. "I'm sorry for bumping into you like that," she said, her voice nervous. But Mr. Redd didn't mind her embarrassment. He was more interested in her beauty when he first saw her before she ran away.

"I couldn't stop thinking about you," he said. "Has anyone ever told you how beautiful you are?"

Emily blushed again. She tried to hide her face from him, but Mr. Redd turned her face towards him.

"You don't need to hide from me," Mr. Redd said. "Your body says more than just your words."

Emily was utterly embarrassed. She didn't want to look at his face. "You must think I'm a clutz," she said. "All the other students at my college tell me all the time."

But Mr. Redd disagreed with her. "I don't think you're clumsy," he said. "You have such a remarkable body. I would love to see something that accentuates your beauty more."

Emily tucked the lock of her messy hair behind her ear as she looked at her raggedy hand-me-down clothes before returning to Mr. Redd. "I don't own anything that makes me look pretty," she said. "I'm just an ugly little rag doll. These clothes you see me wearing are my old, raggedy hand-me-downs from my parents."

Mr. Redd didn't care about her clothes or the fact that they were hand-me-downs. "Clothes don't make the woman," he said. "It's what's underneath that makes you beautiful."

Emily didn't believe him. She thought he was lying to her. But he wasn't. He was more interested in her beauty and imagined how wonderful she would look in something elegant.

"I don't mind what you wear," he said. "You are a woman. That's what makes you special."

He handed her a card with his name and phone number on it. "My card," he said.

The card read, "Mr. Lucien Redd, CEO, Redd Enterprises Inc. Phone: 704-623-4896."

Emily had never heard of Redd Enterprises or that its CEO was him.

"Turn the card over," Mr. Redd said.

So she did.

On the back, it read: "Redd Enterprises Inc. Specializes in economic development, intelligence, and communication. Our primary focus is on acquiring the best companies and supporting those in the community who are the most in need."

Emily was impressed. "Sounds like a big business," she said.

"I know," said Mr. Redd. "If you ever want to see me, please visit my office," he added. Then he left the coffee shop, telling Emily he would see her again whenever she wanted to call him. He got into his dark red stretch limousine parked outside and drove away.

Emily was left staring at the sight of Mr. Redd's limo. His charm enamored her. "He must be rich," she thought. But she shrugged off the thought, knowing he would never go with someone like her. She sighed deeply and went straight home.

Later that evening, Emily was in bed trying to sleep. But she couldn't stop hearing his voice in her head. He had called her beautiful, even though she had never been considered pretty by anyone else in town, not even by her family. She looked up at the ceiling and sighed.

As she closed her eyes, the image of Mr. Redd appeared. Now she knew the name of the mysterious man she had been imagining. But now she had a problem: did he call her "beautiful" because he liked her, or was there something about her that drew him to her? Whatever it was, Emily didn't want to be bothered with it. She put that thought aside and went to sleep, having already had enough excitement and fear for one day.

# Chapter 3

The next day, at Halo University, Emily was in the computer lab, browsing pictures of Redd Enterprises on the internet. On the screen, she saw a 60-story building of red-tinted windows. Next, Emily looked at some photos of Mr. Redd. She was so intrigued by Mr. Redd that she had to get to know him. Just then, Jetta, Nicole, and Katie approached her.

"Well, if it isn't the ugly mudball," said Nicole. "What are you looking at?"

Emily frowned at the three college girls. "I'm doing some research on the computer," she said. They looked at her with confusion at first. Then, they started laughing at her. Emily didn't like being laughed at by the college girls. But then, Nicole looked at the pictures on the screen.

"Who is that guy?" she asked.

Emily told them that the man in the photographs was Mr. Redd.

The college girls gasped in surprise.

"You mean *THE* Mr. Redd of Redd Enterprises Inc.?" said Jetta.

"Yes," said Emily. "I met him yesterday at the coffee shop Downtown. He helped me clean up a mess I had made. He said I was beautiful."

The college girls laughed at Emily again.

"You? Beautiful?" said Nicole jokingly. "Why would he say you're beautiful? You don't even come close to being "pretty." But Emily didn't believe them. It was the first compliment she had received from a man, and she took pride in it.

"Maybe he likes me," she said.

Nicole didn't believe her. She thought she was making it up to impress them. "Likes you?" she said. "Look at you. You don't have a chance with someone as handsome as Mr. Redd."

Emily looked at her with a confused expression on her face. "What makes you say that?" she said.

"Mr. Redd is a multi-billionaire," Nicole said. "He's the wealthiest entrepreneur in the world and has no time for romance with someone like you. He only goes for the rich, pretty, and popular girls like us. Which, by the way, you are **NOT**!"

It made Emily feel disappointed to hear her say those words. But she changes her attitude. "Maybe he might ask me out on a date," she said. "I have his phone number." She pulled out the card Mr. Redd gave her and showed it to them as proof. But Nicole disapproved of the card and called it a fake.

"I don't believe you," she said. "There is no way Mr. Redd would ask someone like you out on a date. He doesn't want to be with someone like you! My advice: stay away from him before you get hurt."

Nicole punched Emily in her left arm before leaving the computer lab with Jetta and Katie.

Feeling hurt, Emily stood up and called out to them. "One day, you will see me in Mr. Redd's limo arriving at the college," she shouted.

The college girls stopped and turned to face her. Nicole approached Emily and slapped her in the face. "I don't think so," she said. "Because that day will never happen for you. Freak!" Then, she turned around and rejoined Jetta and Katie.

The three college girls leave the lab, leaving Emily with a bruised mark on her arm and a slap in the face. She didn't like being called a "freak." She wasn't going to take such ridicule from those three college girls. She would prove them wrong about Mr. Redd's taste in women.

The following day, Emily was at home, sitting by the telephone in the living room while her parents went shopping with Marcus. They were buying new sneakers for his next basketball game, which was coming up next month.

Emily was examining the card Mr. Redd had given her. She wrestled with the thought of calling him, but the words Nicole told her echoed in her head. "There is no way Mr. Redd would ask someone like you out on a date." Emily's mind needed to decide whether to call him or not. So, without hesitation, she decided to call him. However, she worried that he might not like her. She didn't want him to think she was desperate. She picked up the phone and dialed the number. On the phone, she heard Mr. Redd's voice talking.

"Hello," he said. Hearing his voice on the other line made Emily's heartbeat. She couldn't keep it quiet.

"This is Emily Richards," she said.

Mr. Redd was talking from his suite at the Bella Rose Hotel. He was in the living room, listening to Classical music. He was happy to receive a call from Emily.

"So nice of you to call me," said Mr. Redd.

Emily began to ask him about his taste in women. "What do you think about women who are not pretty or popular?" she asked.

Mr. Redd laughed heartily. "What made you ask that question?" he said. Then, Emily told him that three college girls told her that he didn't like girls who were ugly and unpopular like her. But Mr. Redd didn't believe her.

"I think those girls were just jealous," he said. "They don't know you like I do."

Emily did need clarification on what he meant. "I just met you one day," she said.

"But I want to get to know you better," Mr. Redd said. Then, he asked Emily if she would like to go on a date with him tonight. "Perhaps you would like to join me for dinner tonight," he said.

Emily was surprised to be asked out on a date by the handsome Mr. Redd. "Are you asking me out on a date?" she asked.

Mr. Redd laughed. "Of course I am," he answered. "Do you want to go on a date with me?"

Emily thought about it at first. But then, she remembered what Nicole and the other girls said about Mr. Redd asking her on a date.

"I can't," she said.

"Why not?" Mr. Redd asked.

Emily told Mr. Redd about what the college girls said to her the other day. "They said you don't have time for romance with someone like me," Emily replied. "They said I should stay away from you before I get hurt." She sounded disappointed as she said those words to Mr. Redd. But Mr. Redd told her to forget what those college girls said to her.

"I don't care if you're ugly or pretty," he said. "I just want you to go on a date with me. Forget about those naysayers. Let the woman in you come out. You deserve some happiness."

Emily was shocked to hear Mr. Redd's words. She thought he would play a joke on her to humiliate her in front of everyone. But then, Mr. Redd added that this was no joke. Then, she thought about disproving the college girls' assumption that Mr. Redd dated only pretty girls.

"Okay, I'll go on a date with you," she said. "When can I see you?"

Mr. Redd told her the time and date for their meeting. "How does 7 pm sound?" Mr. Redd asked.

Emily nodded. "I can do it at 7:00," she answered.

Mr. Redd smiled at Emily's answer. "I'll see you tonight," he said. "Can I have your address?"

Emily smiled. She told him the address of her house, where he would meet her. "2435 Grovedale Street, Halo Town," she said. She said "goodbye" to Mr. Redd and hung up the phone.

She was happy to be going on a date with a man. An actual date with a man, not a pretend one for her. She wanted to jump up and scream with joy. But then, her parents came home.

"We're back," Mr. Richards said.

Emily saw her parents and Marcus go into the house with their hands full of bags. They hardly noticed Emily standing in the living room. Then, Marcus approached her with a look on his face.

"Sorry you didn't get to go shopping," he said sarcastically. "Next time, when you want to buy baby clothes for yourself." He turned around and headed to the kitchen to help Emily's parents unload the bags for dinner. Emily wasn't going to let her brother's words stop her. She had a date with Mr. Redd tonight. So she went upstairs to get ready.

That evening, Emily was taking a shower. She was imagining her date with Mr. Redd. Emily wanted it to be perfect. As she stepped out, she dried herself off with a clean towel. Emily headed into her room to get herself ready. She fixed her wet, flat hair by brushing it and making it appear stylish. Next, Emily went to her closet to find something nice to wear. But she couldn't find anything in her closet. All she could see was a pale blue sweater dress with a turtleneck. It wasn't fancy or elegant, but good enough for her. She paired her sweater dress with a pair of black flat shoes. She looked at herself in the mirror. But all she could see was the plain, ordinary, ugly duckling in a pale blue dress with a bird's nest of hair. Then, she looked at the clock. It was already 6:58 pm—two minutes to 7:00.

"Oh no," she said. "I'm going to be late." Emily quickly grabbed her brown handbag and headed downstairs.

Emily began to leave her house, but Marcus caught her as she was going out the door. He was standing outside the kitchen with a glass of milk and a plate of chocolate chip cookies.

"Where do you think you're going?" he said.

Emily looked at him nervously. "Marcus," she said. "What a surprise."

Marcus put the milk and cookies on the table and looked at Emily in her sweater dress. Marcus asked, "Why are you dressed like that?"

Emily swallowed. Emily swallowed, then confessed to him. "I got a date with a man," she said.

Marcus laughed. "You got a date with a man?" he said.

"Yes," Emily replied, nodding. "His name is Mr. Lucien Redd. He's the wealthiest man in the world and the CEO of Redd Enterprises Inc. He asked me for a date, and I'm meeting him tonight."

Marcus didn't believe her. He thought she was talking wildly to make herself memorable.

Then, Marcus began to call her parents. "Mom, Dad, Emily's got a..." he shouted. Emily tried to stop him by covering his mouth with her hands.

"Don't tell Mom and Dad," she whispered. "I don't want them to know."

Marcus took her by her arms and led her back to her room. "You can't go out on a date," he said. "Mom and Dad will blow their tops over you." But Emily didn't want to go back upstairs. She would meet Mr. Redd tonight at 7:00 pm and didn't want to keep him waiting. Marcus blocked her by standing in front of her with his body. "I can't let you go without Mom and Dad's consent," he said. "Besides, he could be a heartbreaker, pursuing you for your affection." Emily didn't believe him.

"I just met him," she said. "He's nothing like that. He said I was beautiful." Marcus explained to her that all men like Mr. Redd are like that.

"They wine and dine women first," he said. "But then, they deceive them by breaking their hearts afterward."

Emily didn't want to hear another word out of her brother. She pushed him out of her way and headed to the front door. At the same time, the doorbell rang. As Emily opened the door, Mr Redd stood in the doorway. He wore a black casual suit, a dark gray shirt, and no tie. Emily's eyes grew wide with wonder at the sight of him standing before her. He looked incredibly handsome.

"Good evening," he said, smiling. "It's great to see you." He looked at Emily in her sweater dress. Emily thought he wouldn't like her in something plain and boring. But Mr. Redd didn't mind. He liked her because she was beautiful. "What a lovely dress you're wearing," he said.

Emily looked at him, confused. She hid her face in shame. Mr. Redd reached out his hand and pulled her face to meet him. "Why so shy?" he asked. "You shouldn't hide such a beautiful face from me."

Emily nervously bit her bottom lip, making Mr. Redd's eyes widen. He looked at her hungrily, thinking about how her lip would taste if he bit into it. "You are indeed the most beautiful woman I've ever seen," he said. Emily blushed again. But then she lowered her head. Emily was feeling embarrassed.

"No one has said I was beautiful before," she said.

"Good thing I'm the first," Mr. Redd said.

"You wouldn't want me," Emily said. "I'm too odd and unattractive. I'm ugly."

But Mr. Redd laughed. "No, you're not," he said. "Such a lovely thing like you shouldn't hide yourself from the world. You have such radiance that makes you stand out. Something about you sparks a flame."

Emily shook her head in disbelief. "I'm just a college student," she said. Mr. Redd thought she was more than just a college student. He saw her as something more, so much more.

"Shall I take you to my car?" he asked.

Emily lifted her head. "You have a car?" she asked.

Mr. Redd replied, "Yes." He showed her his car parked outside her house. It was a black Ford Mustang with a red interior. The license plate read: "REDD" in capital letters. "How else do you think I would have gotten here?" he said.

Emily's eyes grew wide. "Am I dreaming?" she said.

"You're not dreaming," Mr. Redd said. "This is real. Let me walk you to my car."

Emily was amazed to see a black Ford Mustang. "That's just one of the cars I own," Mr. Redd said. "I own four of them. I also own a limousine. It's the color red. I should call my chauffeur to come by." Emily shook her head. She was okay with getting a ride in a Ford Mustang.

Mr. Redd took Emily's arm and took her to his car. Emily told Marcus she'd be home by 11:00 pm. Marcus was shocked to see his sister on a date with a man. He needed clarification.

As they entered the car, Mr. Redd drove them down the road in the twilight's glow. They drove into town as the lights began to shine. Emily asked Mr. Redd where they were going.

"It's a surprise," Mr. Redd said. "I'm going to show you the time of your life." They arrived at the restaurant La Flamme Rouge, a fancy establishment with a lavish exterior. There were hedges on the outside, extravagant lighting, and fancy décor that elevated high society. Emily couldn't believe her eyes. The place was huge, fancy, and expensive. As Mr. Redd took her inside, she looked at the interior. Soft music played in the background, and the light shone from the candles. Emily was speechless upon seeing the restaurant.

Just then, a waiter showed up. He noticed Emily and Mr. Redd and smiled.

"Your name, please," he said.

"I reserved a table for Mr. Redd and the guest," Mr. Redd replied.

The waiter looked at the reservation list and found his name. "Your table is right this way," he said. He took Mr. Redd and Emily to a table near the back corner of the restaurant, where a candle and a rose were already in place. Emily sat down at the table. Mr. Redd sat next to her on the opposite side. Then, Mr. Redd told the waiter he would like some red wine.

"As you wish, Sir," the waiter said. The waiter walked away to get some wine.

Emily was feeling shy at first. But at the same time, she felt open. It was her first date with a man. It made her feel nervous. Mr. Redd reached out his hand and lifted her face.

"What's the matter?" he asked. "Isn't this your first date with a man?"

Emily nodded in response. "This is my first time," she said. "But I feel a bit nervous."

Mr. Redd asked Emily why she felt nervous on her first date.

"My parents never let me go on a date with a man without their permission," Emily said. "If they see me with a man, they will blow their tops like a volcano."

Mr. Redd laughed at Emily's words. He found her sense of humor astounding. "What do you do for fun around here?" he asked.

Emily sighed. "Nothing," she said.

Mr. Redd raised an eyebrow. "Nothing?" he asked. "Don't you go out to parties or anything?"

Emily told him, "No." She didn't do anything for fun in town. "I only stay home every night," she said.

Emily asked Mr. Redd what he did for fun.

"I'm usually working in my office, " Mr. Redd replied. "But I sometimes enjoy a night on the town: dinner, dancing, parties, nightclubs. Mostly going out to fancy events. But it can be lonely sometimes. It's hard to enjoy an evening if you have no one to share it with. You may want to accompany me to an event."

Emily was not keen on attending evening events with a man. "I wish I could," she said. "Sadly, my parents won't allow me to go out after 7 pm. Halo Town gets pretty rough at night. Strangers emerging from alleyways, places that are always closed by 9 or 10 o'clock, can make the night seem boring. Nothing much to do."

Mr. Redd rubbed his chin, unsure of Emily's words. "Nothing much to do, you say?" he asked.

Emily nodded her head. "Yes," she replied. "There's no excitement for me. Every night is the same. Boring, boring, boring."

Just then, the waiter returned with a bottle of red wine for the two. "Here you are, Sir," he said. "A vintage 1492 wine from Burgundy." He set the bottle down and took two glasses. The waiter popped the cork off the bottle and poured the wine into the glasses.

Then, Mr. Redd told the waiter that he would like to order dinner. "What would you like to have, Sir?" asked the waiter.

Mr. Redd looked at the menu and made his selection. "Two plates of the same meal," he said.

"Excellent choice, Sir," said the waiter, going off to bring their order.

While he was gone, Mr. Redd offered Emily a glass of wine to drink. "Here," he said. "Drink up."

But Emily didn't want any wine. "Sorry, I don't want any," she said. Mr. Redd questioned her why she wouldn't drink the wine. "I'm not of legal age," Emily replied. She was 19 years old and not allowed to consume alcoholic beverages at her age. However, Mr. Redd didn't mind her age; he only cared about her beauty in her blue sweater dress. He set the glass down in front of Emily for her to take. So she took the glass of wine and raised it to her lips for a sip. Mr. Redd watched as she drank the wine. A seductive grin appeared on his face.

As Emily set the glass back down, she looked at Mr. Redd and felt a little dizzy. A hiccup escaped from her mouth. "Hiccup!" she said.

"Are you okay?" Mr. Redd asked.

Emily nodded but also felt woozy from the wine. "I'll be fine," she said. Mr. Redd poured her another glass of wine and made her consume it. Another hiccup escaped from her mouth.

"Hiccup!"

Mr. Redd grinned. "How is it?" he asked.

Emily looked around the room, trying to catch a glance at Mr. Redd. "I feel dizzy," she said drunkenly. The waiter returned with two plates for Mr. Redd and Emily, containing a steak, grilled fish, and steamed vegetables. Emily looked at the plate and was famished.

"Bon appétit," said Mr. Redd.

"Bon appétit," Emily responds. The food tempted Emily, who had never had a fancy dinner before. She began to eat the food and was amazed by the taste.

Mr. Redd placed his hand on her face. "I want to know everything about you," he said.

Emily gulped lightly. "Why do you want to know about me?" she asked.

Mr. Redd wiped his mouth with a napkin before he told her why he wanted to know about her. "People often share things about themselves with me all the time," he said. "Those deep, dark, secret desires on their minds."

Emily put down her knife and fork and began to speak to him. "I'm a college student at Halo University," she said. "But I am a poor, mistreated nobody." Mr. Redd was surprised to hear Emily say those words to him.

"What makes you say that?" he asked.

So, Emily began to explain to him how miserable her life was. "All my life, I have been an outcast," she said. "I struggle with my non-existence every day with no change. Everyone has mistreated me, including my family. All the students on campus make fun of me; the professors make me stay behind to retake my tests while the others go off and have a good time. No guy would want to go out with me because I'm a virgin."

Mr. Redd was surprised to hear Emily say she was a virgin. "Men must throw themselves at you," he said. "How can you be the most beautiful woman in the world and not have a man in your life?"

Emily nodded her head. "My parents don't allow me to have a man," she said. "They're concerned about my innocence. They don't like me. I'm a loser."

Mr. Redd's mind clicked instantly. He realized what he could do to seduce Emily and followed his plan. "You're not a loser," he said.

Emily's eyes began to fill with tears. "I am a loser," she said. "Since the day I was born, I have always been the one left out. At Christmas, on my birthday, and on Thanksgiving. My family hates me." Emily hid her face from Mr. Redd so he wouldn't see her cry.

Mr. Redd took her face and looked into her eyes. "Forget about your parents," he said. "You don't need them."

Emily trembled at Mr. Redd's words. Then, she could feel his hands reaching up to her breasts. She let out a gasp at his touch. Her face turned red from the temptation he was giving her. "I understand how you're feeling," Mr. Redd said. "I can sense it in your body. Every inch of you. The thought of your body in my arms makes me want you."

Emily tried to cheer up, but the tears continued to fall from her eyes. "Look at me," Mr. Redd said. "No need for tears. You are beautiful. That's all that matters. You didn't know that until I met you."

Emily wiped her tears away and tried to smile. But deep down, she still felt miserable. Then, Emily began to tell him her wish. "Can I tell you something?" she asked.

"Certainly," replied Mr. Redd. "You can tell me anything. What is it you desire most?"

"What I would like is a life of luxury," said Emily. It caught Mr. Redd's attention. His eyes grew wide with wonder at Emily's wish.

"Go on," he said.

"I wish to have a life of luxury like a princess," Emily said. "I want to receive gifts, attend parties every night, wear beautiful evening dresses, and be treated like royalty. It has been my lifelong dream. But it never came true because my parents disapproved of my dreams and wishes. They're poor. However, I want to be rich with a lot of money so I can do whatever I want, whenever I want. I want to be like a celebrity."

Mr. Redd was amazed by Emily's words. A glint in his eyes gleamed. "You wish for a life of luxury, you say?" he said. "Well, I can arrange it for you."

Emily asked him what he could do. Mr. Redd told her about how he could make her wish come true. "I can give you a life of luxury," he said. "I will make you the most popular woman in the world. You will be dressed in the most lavish evening gowns and attend parties at all the hot places in town without a curfew."

Emily was amazed to hear Mr. Redd's words about granting her a luxurious lifestyle. "Can you do that?" she asked. Mr. Redd smiled. He handed her a business card with the address of Redd Enterprises Inc. on it.

"Come by my office," he said. "I'll explain everything to you." Emily picked up the card and read it carefully. On the card was the name: "Redd Enterprises Inc., 4661 Crimson Ave., Diablo City."

Emily looked at Mr. Redd as she placed the card on the table. "This is where you're from?" she asked.

"Yes," replied Mr. Redd. "Diablo City, the Capital city of the world."

Emily had never heard of Diablo City before. "How big is this city?" she asked.

Mr. Redd explained Diablo City to her. "Diablo City is quite large," he said. "Theaters, restaurants, penthouse apartments, and casinos."

Emily envisioned Diablo City in her mind. She could see buildings as far as the eye could see. It made her eyes flutter. Mr. Redd continued to tell her about the city. "I have a penthouse there," he said.

Emily gasped. Mr. Redd had a penthouse in Diablo City. It was surprising for her. "You have a penthouse?" she asked.

Mr. Redd smiled at her question. "Yes, I do," he said. "I live in the Luxuria Luxury Apartment, located in the Downtown area of Diablo City. You should come by sometime to see how I live."

Emily needed to decide whether to go to a man's penthouse. She started hesitating at first. Then, Emily began to speak. "I can't," she said. "I'm still in college and don't want to miss any of my classes."

Then, Mr. Redd had an idea. "How about if you came to my office after college that afternoon?" he said.

"Are you sure?" Emily asked. "What about my parents? They could worry about me?"

But Mr. Redd interrupted her for a brief moment, reminding her of what she had said to him before about her family. "Didn't you say your family never liked you?" he said.

Emily thought about it and remembered what she told him. "Of course," she said softly. "I did say that my parents never liked me. But I didn't mean it like that."

Mr. Redd calmed her down by gently touching her chest. "I know what you said," he told her. "Don't worry about it. Your parents will never know."

So, she agreed to visit Mr. Redd tomorrow afternoon after finishing her Halo University classes. Emily went back to eating her dinner before it got cold.

After dinner was over, the two left the restaurant together. Mr. Redd took Emily to his car and drove her home. While in the car,

Mr. Redd turned on the radio to listen to music. Emily heard the radio and asked what type of music it was.

"This is opera," Mr. Redd said. Emily had never heard of opera before. "It's an excerpt from Faust," Mr. Redd said. He was right. The music was from the opera "Faust." It was called "Mephistopheles' Aria" from Act 2. Emily was curious about what "Faust" was. "It's an opera by Charles Gounod," Mr. Redd said. "Perhaps I can take you to see it."

Emily thought about it. "Maybe someday," she said. Mr. Redd smiled as he turned up the radio's volume to hear the music more clearly. They pulled up in front of Emily's house a few minutes later. The lights in the house were off. Her parents were already asleep.

Emily told Mr. Redd she had a wonderful time tonight. "I hope to see you again," Mr. Redd said. Emily felt relieved for the first time going on a date with a man like Mr. Redd. She couldn't wait to tell the college girls about it the next day.

"The girls told me that you don't do romance," Emily said.

Mr. Redd stroked his chin. "You're right," he said. "I'm not a romantic person. I don't do romance, chocolates, or flowers. My tastes are very singular."

Emily had never heard of a non-romantic person before. "You must be pretty boring," she said. Mr. Redd corrected Emily's phrasing.

"Not boring," he said. "Intimidating. I can be persuasive, intelligent, reliable, and controlling."

Emily laughed a little at Mr. Redd's words. "You sound like a control freak," she said.

"You could say that," said Mr. Redd.

After saying "goodnight" to each other, Mr. Redd drove away, and Emily headed inside her house. She was feeling exhausted, yet happy. Emily went into her room and closed the door. She removed her sweater dress, put on her pajamas, and got into bed.

Emily took the card from her handbag and looked at the address. She knew what she had to do. She would have to go to Redd Enterprises after college the next day.

# Chapter 4

The next day, Emily awoke and got dressed. When she came downstairs, she saw her parents in the living room. Mr. Richards turned on the light and looked at Emily with anger in his eyes.

"Where have you been?" he asked.

Emily looked at her parents. "Hi, Mom and Dad," she said. Mr. Richards frowned at her.

"I asked you a question," he said. "Where have you been?"

Emily began to tell her father about her date the night before. "I went on a date with Mr. Redd," she said. "He took me out to dinner at a fancy restaurant in town, and it was wonderful."

Her parents were upset. "You went on a date without telling us?" Mrs. Richards asked.

"Please, Mom," said Emily. "He was quite a gentleman." Emily's Mom and Dad gave her a disappointed look.

"How could you do this?" Mr. Richards said. "Why would you go on a date without telling us first?"

Emily asked them how they had found out about her date with Mr. Redd.

"Marcus told us you went on a date with a man," said Mr. Richards. "You left the house after 7:00 last night despite our instructions not to go out alone at night. What if something were to happen to you?"

Emily told them she was fine and nothing terrible had happened. But they didn't believe her.

"You're not to date any men without our permission," said Mr. Richards.

It made Emily upset. "I'm not a child," she said. "I'm 19 years old."

Mr. Richards yelled at Emily. "Not another word out of you," he said. "Now, get out! You're going to be late again!"

Emily was frustrated. She felt unappreciated by her parents. Just before leaving the house, Emily saw Marcus coming down the stairs.

"So, how was your date with your new boyfriend?" he said. Emily punched Marcus in his arm.

"I can't believe you ratted me out like that," she said. Marcus shook off the pain and started teasing Emily for going on a date without telling her parents.

"You thought I could keep a secret about you from Mom and Dad?" he said. "You're a weirdo, Emmy. You should know better than to go on a date without their permission."

Emily gasped. Being called names by her brother made her angry.

"I didn't ask for their permission," she said. It made Emily angry. She felt her whole family was against her simply because she had met a man. She left the house and went to Halo University to get her mind off her fight with her parents and brother.

That afternoon, Emily left Halo University and headed into town alone. She took out the card from her pocket and called a taxi. When the cab approached, Emily told the driver to take her to Redd Enterprises in Diablo City. She got into the cab and traveled down the road, leaving Halo Town behind.

Thirty minutes later, the taxi arrived in Diablo City. It was a big city full of life and wonder. The town had skyscrapers, office buildings, and penthouse apartments. Emily looked out the window in amazement. She had never seen a city as stunning as this in her life.

Compared to her small-town home, this was a more lavish setting. There were stores, hotels, theaters, a stadium, and casinos.

"Incredible," Emily said.

She was speechless at the vastness of the city. As the taxi stopped in front of the Redd Enterprises building, Emily stepped out and tipped the driver. The cab drove off, and Emily was alone. She looked at the building, and her eyes grew wide. Redd Enterprises Inc. was a large, imposing building with glass windows, steel, and marble. Above the door was a red sign that read: "Redd Enterprises Inc." Emily swallowed as she entered the building through the glass doors.

In the lobby, Emily looked at the interior design. It was vast and full of people in suits. Some were executive workers, others were assistant managers, and some were secretaries. Feeling intimidated, Emily approached the receptionist's desk quietly. The receptionist at the desk was wearing devil horns in her hair. Emily tapped on the desk lightly to get her attention.

"I'm here to see Mr. Redd," she said.

The receptionist looked at her. "Oh yes," she said. Mr. Redd's office was on the 40th floor. Emily nodded, and she made her way to the elevator. As she headed inside, she pressed a button on the wall, which took her to the 40th floor. Emily headed to Mr. Redd's office down the hallway. Her heart was thumping loudly. She placed her hands over her chest to soften the sound. At the doors of Mr. Redd's office, she saw two female secretaries in tight red mini-skirt suits with stiletto heels and silk black thigh-high stockings. Emily was nervous but, at the same time, jealous, seeing how gorgeous the secretaries looked.

Then, she walked up to another receptionist working behind the desk. "I'm here to see Mr. Redd," she said.

The secretary smiled as she looked through the schedule list. "Please wait over on the couch," she said. So she did. Emily went over to the couch to sit down. As she did, she began to look out the window. The view of the city was marvelous. The skyscrapers were as big as Sequoia trees.

"He must enjoy the view a lot," Emily thought.

Two seconds later, the secretary came up to Emily. "Mr. Redd will see you now," she said. Emily got up from the couch and walked up to the Secretary. She guided Emily down the hallway and made their way into his office. The secretary opened the door and led Emily inside. As she entered, Emily saw how lavish and intoxicating his office looked. It was red with paintings hanging on the walls. It was bigger than any office she had seen before. Inside the office, Mr. Redd was sitting at his desk. He wore his dark gray business suit with a crimson tie. He looked charming and professional.

Emily cleared her throat, which got his attention. Mr. Redd looked up at Emily and smiled. "So nice to see you," he said to her. "Please have a seat."

Emily sat down in the red leather chair near the desk. Mr. Redd got up from his chair and walked toward Emily. He kissed her hand and gave her a seductive stare. "What a pleasure to meet you," he said. Emily blushed bright red. Then, he led her to his desk and told her to sit in the leather chair. Mr. Redd stood before her, near his desk, as Emily began to ask him questions about his business as the CEO of Redd Enterprises.

"To what do you owe your success?" she asked. Mr. Redd explained to Emily how successful he had been with his vast wealth as an entrepreneur.

"Business itself," he said. "Business is about people, and I've always loved people. What motivates them, what inspires them." Emily was amazed at how seriously Mr. Redd took business and people.

"You're just lucky," she said.

Mr. Redd smirked at Emily's remark. "I happen to be rich," he said. "Luck has nothing to do with it. I'm a man of luxury. I know what most people want. And I give them exactly what they want. You could say the harder I work, the more luck I get."

Emily's expression changed hearing how lucky Mr. Redd was. "You must be proud to have such a vast empire," she said. "But you're so young. How old are you?"

"I'm 26 years old," Mr. Redd answered. "But age has nothing to do with me. I exercise on a lot of things." Emily was amazed that someone like Mr. Redd could be a multi-billionaire at such a young age. She thought he would appear to be older than 26 years. It was as if he were somewhere in his mid-30s or early 40s.

"How long have you been a multi-billionaire?" she asked.

Mr. Redd laughed. "12 years," he said. "Maybe longer." Suddenly, he stopped. "But enough about me," he said. "Let's talk about you."

Emily looked up at him. "What about me?" she asked.

Mr. Redd went to his desk to discuss his plan with her. "Remember when I said I can make you the most beautiful woman in the world?" he asked.

Emily recalled last night at the restaurant. "Yes, I remember," she said.

"Let me fulfill your dream," said Mr. Redd. "I can make your wish come true."

Emily shook her head at first. "My wish?" she asked.

"Yes, your wish," Mr. Redd replied.

It made Emily curious. "Can you make my wish come true?" she asked.

Mr. Redd smiled at her and raised an eyebrow. "Yes, I can," he said. "That's what I do." He got up from his desk and went around the front. "What if I told you I have the power to grant you that wish?" he said. "A wish that will change your life forever, and you'll never have to be miserable again."

Emily needed clarification on what he meant. Mr. Redd began to explain his deal to Emily. "I will give you a life of luxury with the qualities you require," he said. "The qualities you will receive include new clothes, accessories, private transportation, and invitations to special events I provide. If you agree to accept my deal, I will grant you a life of luxury."

Emily was surprised by the qualities and requirements she would have. Mr. Redd knew she would love the offer she would get if she agreed to accept his deal. "This is a free offer only," he said. "I can give you a life of luxury. But on one condition. You will have to be my assistant."

Emily looked up, completely confused. "Personal assistant?" she asked. She had never been Mr. Redd's assistant before.

"I could use someone like you to tend to my needs," said Mr. Redd. "You are what I'm looking for."

It left Emily feeling confused. "Why do you want me as your assistant?" she asked.

Mr. Redd told her about being a personal assistant. "If you agree to be my assistant, I will offer you a life of luxury," he said. "In return, you will participate in late-night business meetings with me. These meetings include attending evening events."

Emily wasn't sure about it at first. Being Mr. Redd's assistant sounded like an expensive task for her. "Is this like Fifty Shades of Grey?" she asked.

Mr. Redd scoffed at Emily's question about mentioning "Fifty Shades of Grey" to him. "No, it's not," he said. "I've read the book. And to tell you this, I find it boring. There's not enough kinkiness or sex involved. Grey is just a limp-dick submissive trying to be dominant when he isn't. Which explains why he left Anastasia unsatisfied."

Emily thought Mr. Redd sounded funny with his joke. But she remembered that he was a businessman and the CEO of a big company, which meant he was serious. "Your life of luxury will only last for two months," Mr. Redd said. "If this experience is satisfactory, I can make it permanent for you. If this isn't the life for you, I'll cancel our deal, and you'll return to your old, boring life. Agreed?"

Emily smiled. "Okay," she said. "A free offer sounds like a good idea." Just then, Emily realized her college courses. She told Mr. Redd she didn't want to miss her classes.

Mr. Redd told her not to worry. "These business meetings are only at night," he said. "You won't be in any harm at all. Trust me." He gave Emily a tag to wear on her clothes. The tag read, "Personal Assistant."

Emily looked at the tag before looking at Mr. Redd.

"As long as you wear this tag," he said. "You belong to me." Emily needed to figure it out. But Mr. Redd told her what he had told her the night before. "You told me those college girls said you would never get a boyfriend because you were ugly," he said. "But you wanted to prove to them that a guy like me could date someone like you." Emily remembered telling Mr. Redd about her daily non-existence and how the college girls told her that she would never get a man.

Suddenly, a look of determination came into her eyes. If Emily was going to get what she wanted, she would have to agree to Mr. Redd's deal, even if it meant being his assistant.

"I'll do it," she said. "I want a luxurious life with everything I have always wanted. I see even that beautiful red evening gown in the window display daily, coming home from college."

Mr. Redd was amazed to hear Emily agree to his deal. It made him smile as if he knew she would say it. Mr. Redd knew his plan was about to work.

"Very well, then," he said. After the meeting, Mr. Redd got up and took Emily by the hand. They began to leave his office and went to the elevator. The secretaries watched the two of them together in amazement.

As Emily was about to head inside the elevator, she asked Mr. Redd when she would get her life of luxury.

"Just give it time," Mr. Redd said. "You will receive your life of luxury by tomorrow morning. I promise."

Emily smiled, knowing she would get what she wanted. "Can we go on another date?" she asked.

"Absolutely," said Mr. Redd. "We can go on another date. Just as long as I pick the places."

"Thanks," said Emily. "I owe you one. Goodbye."

As the elevator doors closed, Mr. Redd returned to his office, grinning. "You owe me, alright," he said.

Emily and The Devil

Emily left the building and took the taxi back home to Halo Town. As the cab drove off, Mr. Redd watched from his office window. Then, he picked up his telephone and called his secretary.

Later that evening, Emily arrived home. She got out of the taxi and went inside. Then, Emily went upstairs to her bedroom, removed her clothes, and went to bed. After a busy day, Emily sighed. As Emily fell asleep, she began to have a dream about her luxurious life coming true and being with a man she had met. Emily knew Mr. Redd would give her everything she ever wanted and more. She couldn't wait.

The next day, Emily awoke in bed and got dressed. She knew she would be late again, so she didn't want to run into her parents on her way out the door. As she was about to leave, her mother called out her name. Her voice startled her momentarily, but her heartbeat soon returned to normal.

"Good morning, Mom," she said. Mrs. Richards didn't look pleased to see her. She showed Emily a present she had found on the front porch that morning.

"Someone named Mr. Redd left this for you," she said. Emily was surprised to be receiving a present from Mr. Redd. She took the package from her mother and opened it. She was curious to know what was inside. To her surprise, the package was complete with new clothes for her.

There was also a card inside the package. Emily picked up the card and began to read it.

"Dear Ms. Emily Richards," she read. "Consider these clothes a gift from me to you, my assistant. Sincerely, Mr. Redd."

Emily was excited to receive new clothes. She knew that today was going to be a good day for her. Emily went upstairs to change out her hand-me-down clothes and put on the new ones that Mr. Redd had bought for her. She rushed downstairs in her new look. Her mother was surprised but also shocked. She kissed her mother "goodbye" and went out the door with a smile.

When she got to Halo University, Emily happily made her way to class. All the students began to notice her in her new clothes. It was the first time Emily had gained attention from the student body on campus. She felt confident in herself as she was being given attention for the first time. No one was making fun of her or calling her any names. But then, the three college girls show up. They saw Emily's new clothes and started making fun of her.

"Where did you get those clothes from?" said Nicole.

"Did you rob a mall?" asked Jetta.

Emily told them that Mr. Redd bought her those clothes. But they didn't believe her. They thought she stole those clothes to wear and feel like the center of attention.

"Just because you have new clothes doesn't mean you'll get any attention here at Halo University," said Jetta.

"Or anywhere in life," Katie added.

"So just give up, you ugly duckling," said Nicole. "You have no chance in hell of being popular!"

Emily didn't want to be bothered by them. So she left the three college girls and went to class alone.

"Goodbye, girls," she said. Nicole disliked being ignored during conversations because it made her angry.

Throughout the day, Emily felt good and had newfound confidence. She wondered if her new clothes gave her the boost she needed, but she was happy. Emily felt accepted and welcomed rather than spending her life being treated like an outcast. Emily's dancing improved in ballet class, and the other college girls were amazed by her progress. Ms. Welsh was impressed by how good Emily's dancing had become.

"Brava, my dear," she said. "You have improved marvelously." Emily was pleased and was no longer called a clumsy duckling; she was now a graceful swan. After college, she saw the students on her way out of the building, much to the jealousy of the three college girls.

"Who does she think she is?" asked Nicole in a bitter tone. Jetta and Katie were also upset about Emily getting attention from the students.

That afternoon, Emily came home to share her day at Halo University with her parents. She felt happy and proud of how her day had gone. Most of all, Emily wanted to thank Mr. Redd for buying her the new clothes and the red dress.

"Mom, I'm home," she yelled.

As Emily came inside, Mrs. Richards went into the living room. "Emily, is that you?" she asked.

Emily told her mother about her day and how the other students had given her the attention she longed for. Suddenly, Emily noticed a package addressed to Emily sitting on the couch. She opened it to see what was inside. To her surprise, the package contained a red evening gown. Mr. Redd bought her the red evening gown from the window display. Now, it was hers to keep. Emily was thrilled to finally have this dress. Just then, the telephone rang. So Emily went straight to the phone to answer it. It was Mr. Redd calling.

"Hello," he said.

Emily gasped with excitement. She told Mr. Redd that she loved her red evening gown. "Thank you for the gift," she said.

Mr. Redd was happy for Emily. "I can't wait to see you tonight," he said. "I'll come to your house at 7:00."

Mr. Redd was coming to her house to take her on another date. "Okay," she said. "I'll see you tonight." Emily hung up and went upstairs to her room to change out of her clothes.

Later that evening, Emily came downstairs in her red evening dress. She looked like a princess attending her Royal ball. Her parents were surprised to see her in an evening gown they didn't purchase.

"Where did you get that dress?" Mr. Richards asked.

Emily looked at her father with a little twinge of fear. "Mr. Redd bought it for me," she said.

Just then, the doorbell rang. "He's here," said Emily. She quickly went to answer it. She opened the door and saw Mr. Redd standing in the doorway, wearing a dark gray suit and a black shirt.

"Good evening," Mr. Redd said. He looked at Emily in her red evening gown and smiled seductively. "You look beautiful," he said.

Emily blushed as she smiled. "Thank you," she said. "And thank you for buying the dress for me."

Emily's parents were shocked. But they approached him with a smile. "You must be Mr. Redd," Mrs. Richards said. "Emily told us about you."

Mr. Redd smiled. "Yes, I know," he said. "May I say you have such a beautiful daughter?"

Suddenly, Mr. Richards grabbed her arm and pulled her away from Mr. Redd. "Stay away from my daughter, whoever you are," he said, his tone bitter. "You are not welcome here."

Mr. Redd laughed at Emily's Father. He patted him on the shoulder in a friendly manner. "You need not worry about Emily," Mr. Redd said. "She'll be safe with me."

Much to her parents' shock, he wrapped his arm around Emily's waist and pulled her close to his side. Emily's heart was beating. Being this close to Mr. Redd was the best thing that had happened to her. His scent was intoxicating to her. "I'll return to her home tonight at 11 pm," Mr. Redd said.

The two began to head out of the house, closing the door behind them. Mr. Redd took Emily to his car, but it was a limousine—the same one he had driven after leaving the coffee shop. Emily was surprised to see it. The limo was red with black wool tires. Emily's eyes grew wide.

"How did you afford a limo?" she asked.

Mr. Redd laughed. "I am a multi-billionaire," he said. "I'm not ashamed to flaunt my considerable wealth." So, he took Emily inside his limo and joined her. He told the driver to take them into town.

The limo traveled down the road under the glow of Halo Town's twilight. The lights of the town were gleaming like diamonds. Emily had never seen Halo Town at night before. Mr. Redd looked at her with a grin. "See what you've been missing?" he asked.

Emily was in awe. Mr. Redd handed Emily an envelope and told her to open it. Inside was a ticket that read: "Beauche Opera Theater Presents: 'Faust' Tonight at 7 pm."

Emily was surprised. She and Mr. Redd were attending an opera tonight, an experience she had never had before. "I said I was going to take you to see it," Mr. Redd said. Emily was curious whether she would like the opera, but she would try it.

A few minutes later, they arrived at the Beauche Opera Theater in Halo Town to attend the opera. Mr. Redd and Emily stepped out of the car and entered. The theater's grand lobby featured exquisite crystal chandeliers suspended from the high ceiling, casting a shimmering, elegant ambiance. It welcomed guests adorned in their finest, setting the stage for an evening of elegance and enchantment.

Mr. Redd handed the tickets to the usher, and they headed to their seats on the balcony. Emily was initially nervous, but Mr. Redd took her in his arms. "Don't be afraid," he said. "You're in good hands."

Emily smiled. "You're right," she said. All her doubts disappeared as they headed to their seats. As they sat down, the opera was about to begin. Emily asked what the opera was.

"It's Faust," said Mr. Redd. "Do you remember the music I played for you in my car?" Emily remembered the music. The lights dimmed as the music began to play.

As they watched the opera, Mr. Redd touched Emily's thigh with his left hand. He gently squeezed it, causing Emily to squirm in her seat. Mr. Redd shushed her and told her to relax. "Just watch the performance," he whispered. Emily tried to focus on the performance while taking slow, deep breaths. But she was more distracted by Mr. Redd squeezing her inner thigh. She clutched her dress as a wave of pleasure began to wash over her. Mr. Redd noticed her face turning even redder as he gently caressed her. His gentle whisper tickled her ear as he leaned in close. "Does this turn you on?" he whispered.

Emily moaned softly in response. Her eyes fluttered. She bit her bottom lip and pressed her thighs together. Mr. Redd's hand stroked the flesh of her inner thigh up to her waist and then back down again. Emily whimpered from his touch. "Please," she said. "People may be watching us."

Mr. Redd looked around before looking at Emily. "No one's going to notice," he said. "We're up on the balcony." He kissed her neck before returning his gaze to the stage.

Emily tried her hardest to keep quiet, but Mr. Redd's left hand soon began to cup her breasts. He pinched her nipple with his fingers and flicked it rapidly. It was making Emily breathe hard as if she were about to have an orgasm underneath her dress. Mr. Redd smiled at her as he continued pinching and playing with her breasts. Emily told him to stop, but he did not respond. She had no control over herself. Emily gripped the arms of her seat tightly and crossed her ankles. She moaned softly from his touch during the soprano's aria on stage. Her reaction matched the music. She moaned louder and higher from Mr. Redd's touch, who was enjoying hearing her voice the whole time. Mr. Redd was giving her pleasure-seeking fantasy just by touching her erogenous zones, which she never knew she had.

After the opera, they left their seats and headed downstairs to the lobby. They left the theater and walked outside. "That was a tremendous show," Emily said.

"I'm glad you enjoyed it," Mr. Redd said. "Because I did." His hand carefully touched Emily's bottom.

With one squeeze, Emily let out a little squeak. "Oh!" Emily gasped.

Mr. Redd felt her butt on his hand. "You have such a tremendous ass," he whispered. "I can imagine how wonderful it would feel without any clothes on."

Emily giggled, and her cheeks turned red. "I didn't know you had such a reputation with the ladies," she said.

Mr. Redd smiled. "I guess it's my charm," he said. "Ladies can't resist my dashing good looks." They walked to his limo, which was waiting for them. He took Emily inside his limo, and they headed off.

By the time they returned to Emily's house, Mr. Redd kissed her on her lips. It was Emily's first kiss from a man. It was surprising at first. As they stopped kissing, Emily hid her lips from Mr. Redd. Then, she looked at him briefly. "I liked the opera," she said.

"Did you enjoy my touch?" Mr. Redd asked.

Emily blushed when he brought up that moment. His hand touched her breast and flicked her nipple, leaving her having an orgasm on the balcony. She couldn't find the words to express how much she enjoyed it. It made her feel uncomfortable being touched by a man during an opera.

But Mr. Redd laughed. "I was just joking," he said. Emily sighed in relief. Then, she told him it wasn't so bad, but he needed to be more gentle next time he touched her. Emily stepped out of his limo and said "goodnight" to him before heading inside.

"Will I ever see you again?" she asked.

Mr. Redd said, "Yes."

As she entered the house, Mr. Redd watched her from his limo. "Just wait until I see you again," he said. "We've only just begun." A smile appeared on his face. Almost sinister from a distance. He told the driver to drive away down the road. He couldn't wait to see Emily again.

Emily went inside her house and looked out the window. She saw Mr. Redd's limo outside her home as it drove off the street. Emily sighed. She turned away from the window and went upstairs to her room. She could still feel the touch of his hands on her breasts. It was her first experience of being touched by a man. She still felt awkward about how he touched her during the performance. Her face blushed bright red just thinking about it. She didn't know if it was from how he was touching her or the embarrassment from how everyone was watching her in the balcony seats. But she was okay with how he treated her like a gentleman tonight. She began to get undressed and put on her pajamas. Afterward, she got into bed and fell asleep.

The next day, Emily woke up in bed, having had a wonderful dream the night before. Just then, her mother called her downstairs to have breakfast in the kitchen. She got out of bed and got dressed in her new clothes. As she came downstairs to the living room, Emily saw some more gifts addressed to her. They were all sent by Mr. Redd. She opened each one of them individually to see what was inside. To her surprise, there were fancy evening dresses, handbags, high-heeled shoes, and other accessories. Emily was happy to receive some gifts from Mr. Redd. She was beginning to enjoy her life of luxury since her night at the opera, especially in her new red evening gown.

After breakfast, Emily left the house to go to Halo University. But as she came outside, she saw Mr. Redd's limo waiting for her. Emily's eyes grew wide. She would get a ride to Halo University in style like a celebrity. So she said "goodbye" to her mother and got into the limo.

Mr. Redd's limo arrived at Halo University, and Emily exited the campus. All the students stopped to look at her. She looked like a movie star in her fancy attire. Emily smiled as she made her way inside the building. As she did, she ran into the three college girls in the hallway.

"Well, hello, ugly duckling," said Nicole.

"Good morning, girls," said Emily with a wave.

Then, Nicole approached her with a snobbish attitude. "So, how did your date with Mr. Redd go?" she said. "Or not. Because you've never been on a date in your life!"

Jetta and Katie laughed behind her in unison. Emily cleared her throat and explained her date with Mr. Redd to the college girls. "He took me to an opera last night," she said. "He bought me a red evening gown and said I was beautiful."

Jetta and Katie were amazed. "You are so lucky," said Katie.

"He must have treated you like a princess," said Jetta.

But then, Nicole interrupted her. "She's lying," she said. "She's just making this up just to impress us."

But Emily told her she was not making it up. "It's true," she said. "Mr. Redd called me a beautiful princess."

Nicole frowned in disbelief. She didn't even notice the limo Emily came out of. "No way Mr. Redd would date someone as ugly as you," she said in a nasty tone.

Emily was offended. "I am *NOT* ugly," she said.

**"YES YOU ARE!"** Nicole shouted.

Jetta and Katie stopped Nicole from bullying Emily. "Don't call her ugly," they said. Nicole told them to back off. She turned to Emily with a mean look on her face. "Don't think he's going to ask you out on another date," she said. "Because it will never happen. **EVER!**"

They left Emily and headed to class. "This isn't over, Richards," said Nicole. But Emily didn't mind. She loved being called a princess by Mr. Redd. Emily felt very confident. She made her way to class before the bell rang.

Over the next few days, Emily's popularity continued to grow with every passing day. She was getting the attention she deserved. All the students on campus began to treat her like a celebrity. It made her feel happy. She was no longer the plain, boring rag-doll nerd anymore.

Mr. Redd had granted Emily's wish. She got to eat a fancy lunch at the cafeteria with the college guys, earned straight A+ grades in her classes, and received compliments from every student on campus. They began to like her now that she had become popular.

Emily was now the most popular person in Halo Town. Due to her parents' concern, Emily received more gifts from Mr. Redd. But Emily didn't mind her parents. She was getting fame, glamour, accessories, and attention.

She was receiving treatment like a princess out of a fairy tale. She went to the spa daily and received a luxurious treatment provided by Mr. Redd: a full-body massage, a soothing hot tub bath, hair washing, and a manicure. Emily felt like she was in Heaven. She was refreshed, rejuvenated, and feeling good about herself. That afternoon, Emily was at home enjoying her new gifts. She was happy with how her life of luxury was making her. Emily bought herself some new clothes and accessories, including handbags. She looked pretty, like a real woman.

# Chapter 5

Two months later, that afternoon in July, Emily came home to find more gifts waiting for her in the living room. Just then, there was a knock on the door. Emily got up to answer it. Mr. Redd was standing in the doorway. Emily's eyes grew wide at his presence.

"Hello, Emily," Mr. Redd said. Emily was surprised to see Mr. Redd at her house. "May I come in?" he asked. Emily invited him inside and led him into the kitchen.

"Mom, Dad," she called, "Mr. Redd is here." Mr. and Mrs. Richards saw Mr. Redd come in and welcomed him to their home.

"It's a pleasure to meet you," he said. "You must be Emily's father." Mr. Richards gasped.

"Can he stay for dinner?" Emily asked. Her parents were curious if they would allow Mr. Redd to stay for dinner.

"He has no right to be here," Mr. Richards said. Emily felt disappointed. But Mr. Redd approached Mr. Richards and looked him in the eye.

"On the contrary," Mr. Redd said. "I have every right to be here with your daughter."

Mrs. Richards offered Mr. Redd a seat next to Emily. Emily's parents joined their daughter and Mr. Redd at the table for dinner. Mrs. Richards asked Mr. Redd what he did for a living and why he had given Emily all those gifts. Mr. Redd explained that he offered

Emily a life of luxury in exchange for her position as his assistant. Her parents were shocked.

"Our Emily is only a college student," Mrs. Richards said. "She can't be your assistant because she hasn't applied for the job."

Mr. Redd shrugged off the disapproval of Mrs. Richards' words. "I can assure you, Madam," he said. "Your daughter told me that she wished to be like a princess. I said she would have everything she wanted if she agreed to be my assistant."

It almost made Mrs. Richards faint from shock. Mr. Richards got upset. He stood up from his chair and told Mr. Redd to leave. "Emily is too young for a stranger like you," he said. "Take your gifts and leave my house. Stay away from my daughter!"

Emily told her Father to withdraw his words to Mr. Redd, but he didn't. He was serious. Mr. Redd got up from the table and took his leave. Emily was outraged by her parents' actions towards him.

"He was just being nice," she said. Mr. Richards grabbed her arm and brought her towards him.

"That man is not to be trusted," he said. "You should stay away from him." But Emily didn't listen to him. She pulled away from his grip.

"You just don't understand," she yelled. "Mr. Redd was explaining his business as CEO." Mr. Richards frowned. Hearing Mr. Redd's name from his daughter's mouth angered him.

He slapped Emily in the face in a fit of anger. "That's enough!" he yelled. "No daughter of mine is going out with a total stranger!"

Mrs. Richards tried to calm him down, but to no avail. "She's our daughter," she said. "And she's a woman."

Mr. Richards didn't want to hear another word. "Emily is too young to be dating grown men," he said. "She should stay away from him and never leave the house!"

Emily was outraged by her father's words. She threw a plate onto the floor and went upstairs to her room. Emily entered her room and sat on her bed, her face contorted in anger. "Why can't they understand?" she said. "I'm not a child anymore."

The next day, Emily came home from another day at Halo University. She was still upset about what her father said and did the night before. Her parents were not home when she came in. They went out shopping with Marcus again. Suddenly, Emily noticed a package addressed to Emily sitting on the couch. The package had a note that read, "To Emily Richards, from Mr. Redd." Emily sat down to open her package. But when she was about to open it, the telephone rang. Emily put the package down and answered it.

"Hello," she said.

"Hello, Emily," said Mr. Redd, calling from his penthouse. "So nice to call you. How are you today?"

Emily told Mr. Redd about her day in college. "I took another test," she said.

Then, Mr. Redd stopped her for a minute. He was going to ask her a question. "Do you want to go on another date with me?" he asked.

Emily gasped. She was going on a third date with Mr. Redd. "Of course," Emily said. But then, Emily told him she couldn't go tonight because her parents had warned her about dating without their permission. "They warned me never to date any guys without their permission," she said.

Mr. Redd laughed at Emily's words. He didn't care about what Emily's parents said. He wanted to take Emily on another date. "Everything your parents told you was lies," he said. "I'll see you tonight at 7:00. You'll wear the dress I bought for you. Don't cancel it."

Emily didn't want to disobey her parents again. But she couldn't cancel her date with Mr. Redd because she was his assistant and he expected her to join him.

"Okay," she said. Emily hung up and began to open her package. Inside the box was a long blue cocktail dress with matching slingback pumps. She went upstairs to change. A few minutes later, Emily came downstairs wearing her blue cocktail dress to meet Mr. Redd. Just then, the doorbell rang.

"I'll get it," said Emily. She opened the door and saw Mr. Redd.

"Emily," he said, "it's so lovely to see you." Emily blushed at the sight of Mr. Redd again. "Are you ready for our date?" he said.

Emily lowered her head at first, but then remembered what Mr. Redd had told her on the phone and raised her head. "Yes," she said.

Emily left the house without telling her parents where she was going. Mr. Redd took Emily into his arms and pulled her toward his side. He walked Emily to his car, and they went off down the road. They arrived at the Flamme Rouge for a romantic dinner, just as before. As they sat down at the table, Emily remembered her dinner with Mr. Redd at her house the previous day. Mr. Redd noticed how sad Emily was feeling. He sat closer to her in his chair to comfort her.

"Your parents seem like nice people," Mr. Redd said.

Emily felt embarrassed at first, but she shrugged it off. "Sorry for how my father acted towards you," she said. "What happened yesterday wasn't your fault. It was mine."

Mr. Redd leaned toward Emily and looked into her eyes. "What makes you think it's your fault?" he asked.

Emily turned away in shyness. "My father is not used to seeing me around strangers, especially men," she said. "He thinks I'm still a child. He doesn't understand me at all."

But then, Mr. Redd placed his hand on her leg. Emily blushed at first. "You shouldn't listen to what your father says to you," he said. "He's just trying to scare you. Parents are heartless creatures who shatter the dreams of a woman like you. I won't allow it." Then, he placed his hand on her face and lifted her chin. "You want this life of luxury?" he asked.

Emily nodded her head in response.

"Then, don't let your parents or any of those college girls stop you from fulfilling your destiny," Mr. Redd said. "You deserve some happiness in your life. I can see it in your eyes. I know exactly what you want. All you want is more. I will give it to you if you let me."

Emily smiled again. "Do you mean it?" she asked.

Mr. Redd grinned seductively. "Yes, I do," he said. "If you let me fulfill your destiny, you can have everything you desire. Everything to bring out the woman in you."

Emily wiped her tears away now that her sadness was gone. "I feel better already," she said.

Mr. Redd smiled, too. "That's good," he said. "You should come to my penthouse in Diablo City. I can show you what you've been missing." Without discussing it with her parents, Emily wasn't sure about going to Diablo City. Mr. Redd lowered his hand toward Emily's chest and gently touched her breast seductively. "I can take you there in my helicopter," he said. "It's the best one yet."

Emily's eyes light up. "You have a helicopter?" she asked.

"Yes," said Mr. Redd. "I own a deluxe Eurocopter D-600. The finest helicopter in the world. I use it for Global and Coastal business trips." Emily was amazed to hear about Mr. Redd's helicopter. She had never been on a helicopter ride before. Emily imagined what it would be like to fly in one of them. "If you ever want to visit, please don't hesitate to let me know," Mr. Redd said.

After dinner, Mr. Redd took Emily by her hand like a refined gentleman. "Shall I walk you to my car?" he asked.

Emily giggled at his mannerisms. "Yes, sir," she responded. They left the restaurant and walked back to the car. Mr. Redd returned Emily home a few minutes later.

Emily kissed Mr. Redd on the cheek before getting out of his car. "Thanks for making me feel better," she said. "I'm looking forward to seeing you again."

Mr. Redd grinned as Emily closed the door. "Take care, my dear," he said. "I'll see you again soon."

As they said "goodnight," Emily went inside the house. She sighed with relief as she went upstairs to her bedroom. Emily felt much better after her date with Mr. Redd that she had forgotten about her argument with her parents.

The next day, Emily came home feeling happy. She was going to tell her parents about her great day. When Emily came inside, she found a big package waiting for her on the couch in the living room. It was from Mr. Redd in Diablo City. But as she was about to open her gift, her parents and Marcus surprised her unexpectedly. Emily was confused to see her family welcoming her with a surprise.

"What's going on?" she said. Mrs. Richards explained that it was a party to congratulate her on getting good grades in college.

"We just wanted to show you how proud we are of you," she said. Emily's expression changed. Her family had thrown her a party and given her a present from Mr. Redd, all in one day. She felt happy with how her day was going. She headed into the kitchen to join her family for dinner.

Much to Marcus's jealousy, Mr. Richards presented Emily with a cake and a plate of spaghetti and meatballs. Emily was enjoying her life of luxury. So she began to eat her dinner. After that, Emily had a slice of cake for dessert. She was full but happy to eat something other than spinach and plain white bread for a change. Then, Emily opened her present in the living room. In her package, she found a black floor-length evening dress with thin straps and a thigh slip on the right side. Just then, the telephone rang. Emily answered it.

"Hello," she said. It was Mr. Redd calling.

He asked her how she liked her gifts and her life of luxury.

"I love it," said Emily. She thanked him for buying her new clothes and accessories.

Then, Mr. Redd told her he was taking her for a ride in his helicopter tonight. Emily gasped. She thought about it before giving Mr. Redd her answer.

"I'd like to go with you on a helicopter ride," she said.

"My chauffeur will take you to the Helicopter Depot downtown," said Mr. Redd. "I'll be waiting for you on the roof."

When the call ended, Emily was overjoyed. She told her parents she was going with Mr. Redd for a helicopter ride tonight. At first, she thought they would be disappointed. But they weren't. Instead, they let her go on the helicopter ride with Mr. Redd while they stayed here to clean up. Emily hugged her parents before going upstairs to change out of her clothes and put on her black evening gown.

That evening, Emily came downstairs in her black evening dress and matching shawl. "Goodbye, Mom," she said. "I'll see you later." She left the house and found Mr. Redd's limousine waiting outside, as it was this morning. She saw a man stepping out of the limo; it was Mr. Redd's Driver. He wore a dark gray suit with a matching hat. A pin on his jacket read, "Mr. Redd's driver" in capital letters.

"Miss Emily Richards," the driver said. "Your ride is here." He invited Emily inside, and the limo drove off down the road. The limo arrived at a helicopter depot pad downtown in Halo Town. Mr. Redd's servant took Emily out of the limo and brought her to the elevator. They headed to the roof, where they saw Mr. Redd's helicopter. It was a red Eurocopter with the words "Redd Enterprises Inc." in black on the sides.

Emily was shocked. She had never seen a red helicopter before. Just then, Emily saw Mr. Redd standing next to it. He wore a dark red suit with a gray colored shirt and a black necktie.

"Ms. Emily," he said. "Good evening." He took her hand and led her towards the door. He opened the helicopter door for her to step inside. As she did, Mr. Redd secured the door closed. Mr. Redd got in and took the helicopter driver's seat. He closed the door next to him and put on his headset. Mr. Redd offered Emily a headset, and she put them on. Next, he secured her in a seatbelt harness.

"No escaping," he said. Mr. Redd radioed to the console for takeoff. "This is D-600 requesting departure from Halo Town to Luxuria, Diablo City," he said. The helicopter blades started up.

The voice on the other end of the line responded. "Tower Luxuria to D-600; you are clear for departure," said the voice on the console. The helicopter took off into the sky. Emily looked out the window at the ground below disappearing.

Through the sky, they flew to Diablo City at night. Emily looked out of the window and saw the city below. It was beautiful. Diablo City was enormous, illuminated in the twilight dusk. Skyscrapers and penthouses were glowing in the evening air. All the lights seemed to welcome her to the city's nightlife. Emily was in awe of the sight. It was a combination of New York and Los Angeles all in one. The view was marvelous from a bird's-eye view.

Mr. Redd turned to look at Emily. "Enjoying the view?" he asked.

"It's incredible," replied Emily.

Mr. Redd smiled as he continued to fly over the city. "When you fly by night," he said. "You fly blind."

A few minutes later, they arrived at the Luxuria Penthouse. "D-600 coming in for a landing," Mr. Redd said into the microphone. The helicopter landed on the penthouse's roof. As the helicopter blades stopped spinning, Mr. Redd unbuckled Emily from her harness and removed her headset. He opened the door and escorted her out of the helicopter.

Emily felt like she had been on a rollercoaster ride. Mr. Redd took her in his arms and led her to an elevator. They took the elevator down to Mr. Redd's penthouse on the 31st floor. As the doors opened, Mr. Redd brought Emily inside.

"Welcome to my home," he said. "Please make yourself comfortable."

Emily couldn't believe her eyes. His penthouse was more significant than his hotel suite back in Halo Town. "Oh my gosh!" she said. The lavishness of the place blew her away. It was spacious and filled with lush furnishings, a bar in the kitchen, a grand piano, and numerous paintings on the walls. "Nice place for a multi-billionaire," she said. "I wish I had a luxurious penthouse like this one."

Mr. Redd smiled at her. "You want to see more?" he asked. Emily responded with a nod. Mr. Redd showed her around his penthouse. Every room enthralled her. From the living room to the bathroom down the hallway. The office across the hallway was where Mr. Redd worked when he was not at work. The dining room featured a table that seated eight guests. Emily loved his place. "It gets even better," Mr. Redd said. He took her to the balcony to show her the city's view. As he did, Emily was genuinely amazed by the city skyline.

"Halo Town has nothing compared to this," she said.

"It's beautiful," Mr. Redd said. "The city at night is the view I enjoy seeing."

Emily gazed at the city's lights below, which resembled twinkling stars in the night sky. "It's amazing," she said.

"Look over there," Mr. Redd said, pointing to a red light district on the left.

Emily looked closely at the red light district. It looked like a devil's pitchfork. "What is that?" she asked.

"Pitchfork Road," Mr. Redd said. "It's one of my favorite places to go for entertainment. Some call it 'the Devil's Playground' due to its red lights."

Emily was curious. "What's it like down there?" she asked.

Mr. Redd smiled at her. "People go there for nights of debauchery," he said. "Maybe I should take you there one day if it's alright with you."

Emily smiled back and nodded.

He took Emily back inside and sat her down on the couch. He turned on soft music and brought a bottle of wine and two glasses. He poured her a glass and joined her on the sofa.

"You love my lavish penthouse?" he asked.

Emily responded, "Yes." She looked up at his eyes. "I love it so much," she said. "You have such a lavish lifestyle. I wish I could live here with you forever. I think I love you."

Mr. Redd put the glass down and looked at Emily. "You can if you want," he said.

"I can?" Emily asked.

"Yes, you can," Mr. Redd whispered, his eyes filled with longing. "I've been waiting for you for a long time."

Emily opened her eyes. "You've been waiting for me?" she asked. Mr. Redd nodded.

"Yes," he said. "I crave your presence, yearning to possess you completely. You are all I want, all I need."

Emily looked at him with a confused expression. Mr. Redd had been waiting for her. Mr. Redd brought Emily to a mirror on the wall and caressed her body seductively. "Think about it, Emily," he said. "Remember what you told me at the restaurant the other night?" Emily gasped as Mr. Redd's hands began to grope her in places she never knew. "You wanted to be treated properly like a Princess," Mr. Redd said. "I can arrange it for you. Everything you dream of will come true. No one will make fun of you again. No one will hate you. No one will ignore you. Everyone will love you: Emily Richards, the Princess of Luxury. You will have access to all the finest necessities the world has to offer. All you have to do is make a deal with me, and I will give you everything you desire."

Emily felt completely seduced by Mr. Redd's words. They were like the wine she consumed. It left her feeling lightheaded and drowsy. "Just imagine," said Mr. Redd in a low, sexy voice. "I can see you on a bed of silk sheets, satin pillows, and soft velvet blankets. Waking up in the morning in a long, sheer nightgown. Served breakfast every day. I can see you wearing the most beautiful clothes as you walk down the street. Every man in town admires your beauty. Don't you want it?"

Emily closed her eyes as Mr. Redd's hands slowly caressed her body seductively. The two returned to sit down on the sofa. Mr. Redd sat next to Emily. Then, he kissed her on the neck and placed his hands on her body. He kissed her as he caressed her body. Then, he pulled away. "I have a little something for you," he said. "Wait here."

Mr. Redd got up from the sofa and took out a red envelope. When he came back, he handed her the envelope as he sat on a chair beside the couch. "Here," he said. "Open it."

Emily looked at the envelope with a confused look on her face.

"What is this?" she asked.

"This is a contract," Mr. Redd said. Emily had never seen a contract before.

"Why are you giving me a contract?" she asked.

Mr. Redd smiled as he told her not to worry. "There's nothing sinister here," he said. "It's all standard boilerplate. Everything I said, and more, is in there."

Emily needed clarification as to why Mr. Redd would give her a contract.

"I have grown to like you, Emily," Mr. Redd said. "You are the first woman to appreciate my fabulously luxurious lifestyle, and I would like you to consider a deal with me."

Emily looked at the contract before she asked another question. "Why do you want me to make a deal with you?" she asked.

"I want to unlock your dark, deep desires for pleasure, excitement, luxury, passion, and lust," Mr. Redd said. Emily needed clarification on what he meant.

"Is this a joke?" she asked.

Mr. Redd explained to Emily that this was not a joke. He was serious. "I said that I would make your life of luxury permanent if you like this experience," Mr. Redd said. "Open it and read it at your leisure."

Emily opened the envelope, which contained a 500-page contract. She pulled it out and began to read it. The agreement stipulated that Mr. Redd would provide Emily with a life of luxury, including gifts and private transportation to various places she desired, without requiring her to walk. But then, Emily stopped for a second and looked at Mr. Redd.

"I'm not sure about this," she said.

Suddenly, Mr. Redd told her the payment she must make for her luxurious life. "All the luxury made for you is going to cost you," he said.

"What's this going to cost me?" she asked.

"Money is not the best charge," said Mr. Redd. "I'm not asking for cash. Not even a penny. It's something of yours I want. Something precious you must give me."

Emily wasn't sure what he wanted her to give him. "What do I have to give you?" she asked.

Mr. Redd leaned in towards her with a severe expression. "Your soul," he said in a deep voice.

Emily gasped. "My soul?" she said. "I'll have to give you my soul?"

"Absolutely," said Mr. Redd with a smile. "I want you to give me your soul, and I'll give you your life of luxury."

Emily was initially shocked because this was not something she would usually agree to. "I can't give you my soul," she said.

"But you said you owed me one," Mr. Redd said. "I heard you before you left my office."

Emily looked at him and remembered what she had told him a few months ago. "But it's my soul," she said. "Why would I give you my soul?"

Mr. Redd cleared his throat and asked her a question. "You've heard of losing your virginity?" he asked.

"No," Emily said. "My parents wouldn't allow me to lose my virginity to a man."

Then, Mr. Redd began to explain about virginity and her soul. "A soul is like one's virginity," he said. "It's their innocence. Pure, untouched, and useless. When people have sex, they lose their innocence without realizing it—the same thing with souls. Once you lose your soul, you won't know it's gone. Think of it as losing your baby tooth. Only your baby tooth goes to me."

Emily's eyes narrowed. "Well, if it's so useless," she said. "Then, why do you want it so much?"

Mr. Redd didn't want her to be uncomfortable. He changed the subject to ensure that Emily understood the contract terms clearly. "How about I throw in a sweetener?" he said. "Once a week, we visit a place you choose on a predetermined date, just like a regular couple. Movies, theater, dancing. You decide."

Emily thought about it at first. "We can go anywhere I choose?" she asked.

Mr. Redd smirked. "After you agree to my terms," he said. "A life of luxury for one piddling little soul. What other choice do you have? All you have to do is sign."

Then, Mr. Redd handed her a pen shaped like a devil's pitchfork. Emily asked, "Where should I sign the contract?"

Mr. Redd showed her where to sign it. "Here," said Mr. Redd. So Emily took the pen and signed her full name in red ink.

"Emily Abigail Richards," she wrote.

Mr. Redd smiled with delight. "Excellent," he said.

After signing the contract, Mr. Redd got off the couch and extended his hand towards Emily. "Come with me," he said. He took Emily by the hand and led her down the hallway to his bedroom.

"Where are you taking me?" she asked.

"I have a surprise for you," Mr. Redd said. As soon as he opened the door, he turned on the lights and showed her what was inside. "This is my bedroom," he said. In his bedroom, there were red lights and a king-size bed. It was big enough to fit four people. "This bed is where I sleep," Mr. Redd added. "And it will be your bed to sleep in with me." He took her over to his bed and sat her down. Then, he closed the door behind him and locked it. He walked towards her in a slow, sexy manner.

"Emily Richards," he said. "Tonight, you and I will cross the threshold of innocence. Past the point of no return. Let me make you into the woman you long to be."

Emily was curious to know what he would do to her. "Are you gonna make love to me?" she asked.

Mr. Redd gave her a look. "I don't make love," he said. "I fuck. Hard."

His words startled Emily to hear him say the F word to her. Mr. Redd ran his hands up his body before reaching the button on his shirt. "You will embrace it as I have," he said. "There is no holding back, my dear. No resistance, no restraint. Relax, my dear."

Emily swallowed nervously. Seeing a man about to strip in front of her was not something she had expected. "What are you going to do?" Emily asked.

Mr. Redd came closer to Emily as he began to strip slowly. "First, I'm gonna take that little dress off of you," he said. "Then, I will know that you are completely naked underneath. Next, I'm going to pin you to my bed so you won't escape. And finally, I'm going to fuck you so hard you will lose your innocence. You will no longer be a virgin. I will fuck you right here in this bed."

Mr. Redd began to undress himself.

He removed his jacket and tossed it on the floor.

Mr. Redd unbuttoned his shirt to reveal his hard, sexy chest, abs, and biceps.

He removed his pants and shoes.

He stood in front of Emily, completely naked. Emily blushed at the sight of Mr. Redd in the nude. "Oh my God," she said in a raspy voice. But Mr. Redd told her not to mention God in his presence. His hands slowly touched his own body before reaching out towards Emily. She wanted to cover her eyes, but Mr. Redd stopped her. He picked her up and began to kiss her on the lips. Her body was feeling warm. His hands then caressed her body from top to bottom. She was quivering under his touch. Mr. Redd removed her dress and tossed it away. Underneath, she wore a white bra and cotton briefs, which were not the most attractive. But Mr. Redd removed them. As he did, he began to caress and fondle her breasts. His touch made Emily shiver. He kissed her neck and down her collarbone before reaching her chest. His mouth rested on Emily's left breast as Mr. Redd began to lick her nipple until it hardened. He transitioned over to her right breast and repeated the same process. Next, he went from her chest to her stomach until he reached her thighs.

Emily felt warm that she allowed Mr. Redd to sample her innocence. He kissed and licked her inner thighs before making his way to her womanly area. Gripping her hips with his hands, Mr. Redd forced his tongue into Emily's part and began to lick her like honey in a beehive. He could hear the sound of her moans escaping from her mouth. Mr. Redd continued to lick her greedily. Emily moaned louder from feeling his tongue circling her clitoris. Her legs felt weak from the sensation. Mr. Redd stood up towards her and kissed her again. He put her back down on the bed, grabbed her wrists, and brought them up over her head to pin her down. Then, Mr. Redd positioned himself on top of her and began to engage in sexual intercourse with her. He spread her legs open as he inserted his dominant manhood inside her.

Emily gasped and sighed as Mr. Redd penetrated her on the silken seats of his bed. She had never had anything like this. But she was feeling hot all over. Mr. Redd was deflowering her in his bedroom for the first time. He kissed Emily more as he continued penetrating her. His rhythm matched his breathing. It was the most erotic scene Emily could imagine.

"Is this what you want?" Mr. Redd asked.

Emily nodded her head at first. But Mr. Redd wanted her to say "Yes" in response. He penetrated her much harder this time. "Do you want this?" He asked.

At last, Emily said, "Yes." They continued having sex all night. The heat between them was intense, with every wave of pleasure washing over them repeatedly like an ocean of lust. Emily cried out with every thrust Mr. Redd gave her. She could no longer contain herself. Mr. Redd tightened his grip on her wrists more as he continued thrusting into her deeper and deeper. His hips began to hit Emily faster and faster. The bedpost was hitting up against the wall with every penetration given. Both Emily and Mr. Redd let out cries of pleasure in the room until, at last, they reached an orgasm.

When it was over, Mr. Redd removed himself from Emily's body and lay beside her on the bed. Emily was still shaking from her first orgasm. Her body was tired. Yet it still felt warm. Her breathing slowed slightly as her eyes began to close.

Mr. Redd looked at her for a brief minute before kissing her once more. He removed her wrists from the bedposts to let her arms rest.

"Signed, sealed, and delivered," he said at last. "Now you belong to me, Emily Richards."

He licked her body from the bottom to the top as his right hand cupped her breast. He let Emily sleep as he went off to shower in the bathroom down the hall.

Emily slept all through the night after her first night of sexual pleasure with Mr. Redd.

# Chapter 6

The next day, Emily awakened in Mr. Redd's bed. But there was no Mr. Redd. He wasn't here. But then, she noticed her dress was gone, and she was completely naked. She was confused.

"What happened?" she said to herself. She looked around the room in a state of panic and shock. She quickly got out of bed and scrambled to find her dress. She needed to get out of there before Mr. Redd came back. But it was too late. Mr. Redd entered the room fully dressed in a red suit with a white shirt underneath. He was holding a bottle of wine and two glasses.

"Good morning," he said with a smile. Emily looked up and gasped. He was looking at her completely naked. She blushed with embarrassment and tried to cover herself, but to no avail.

"Don't look at me," she said. "I'm naked."

Mr. Redd approached her and pulled her close. He growled seductively. "You do have such a beautiful body," he said. "I would love to see you flaunt those lovely curves all day."

Emily pushed him away and regained her composure. "What happened last night?" she asked him.

Mr. Redd grinned. He told her not to worry. "What happened last night was just between us," he said. "You had a little too much to drink last night. So I took you to my room and got you out of your clothes. I took your innocence to my bed."

Emily gasped. "Are you saying you...That we just...," she said.

Mr. Redd grinned wickedly. "Yes, Emily," he responded. "I fucked you, and you are now mine. Mine to own. You should thank me for that." He handed her a glass and poured some red wine into it. She took a sip. Emily put down the glass and tried to find her dress and shoes. But Mr. Redd stopped her. "I have clothes already for you," he said.

"Where?" asked Emily.

He handed her a present wrapped in red with a black bow. "Open it," he said. Emily opened the present and found some new clothes inside. There was a red bra and panty set, a pink silk button-up blouse with a matching scarf, black stockings, a red blazer jacket paired with a mini skirt, and stiletto pumps in her size. He told her to try them on. So he stepped out of the room to let her get dressed.

A few minutes later, Emily emerged from the room, fully dressed in red and pink, looking like a real woman. Mr. Redd was pleased to see her dressed in this manner. She looked nice. Emily was a little shy about being seen by Mr. Redd, dressed in a suit with a miniskirt. Emily's legs were visible under her skirt, and her blouse was tight, exposing her cleavage.

"Do I look okay?" she asked.

Mr. Redd smiled. "Beautiful," he responded. "You look just like one of my secretaries."

Emily felt warm from Mr. Redd's compliment. "Thank you," she said. Then, Mr. Redd got up from the couch and walked towards her.

"There's something I wanna show you," he said. Emily was curious to know what it was. So Mr. Redd walked Emily down the hallway. He was going to give her a surprise.

"Where are you taking me?" Emily asked.

"To my playroom of pleasure," said Mr. Redd.

Emily looked confused. "What playroom?" she asked.

Mr. Redd smiled. "You'll see."

As they arrived, they stood before a door. The door was red with a golden doorknob. Mr. Redd pulled out a key from his pocket and unlocked the door.

As the door opened, Emily was shocked to see what it was. "This is my playroom of pleasure," Mr. Redd said. The room was full of whips, floggers, handcuffs, spanking paddles, and red ropes for bondage. It was a BDSM room. It wasn't a pleasure room at all. Emily's blood ran cold at the sight of all the torture devices he had. "This is just like in Fifty Shades of Grey," she said. She looked at the items on the walls and shelves. There was a whipping bench and a bondage cross. "Why did you bring me here?" Emily asked.

"To please me," Mr. Redd responded. He slammed and locked the door and began to unbutton his shirt. Emily gasped as Mr. Redd approached her, his eyes filled with a ravenous hunger. Removing his shirt, he set Emily down on a leather-whipping bench.

"Why do I want to please you?" she asked in a small, frightened voice.

"There's something you should know, Emily," Mr. Redd said. "I'm a sadistic dominant."

Emily gasped. She's never heard of a sadistic dominant. "What does that mean?" she asked.

"Let me explain," Mr. Redd said. "I derive pleasure from inflicting pain and suffering on willing partners sexually in exchange for consensual power. I perform BDSM to women who want to be dominated by me."

Emily was curious and asked what BDSM stood for. "BDSM stands for bondage and discipline, dominance and submission, and sadism and masochism," Mr. Redd replied. "I get pleasure from causing pain to others physically."

Emily was frightened to hear what Mr. Redd does to women, considering the disturbing items he has in his room. It was like he owned some sex dungeon in his penthouse. "What does all of this have to do with me?" she asked.

"I've been wanting you to be my submissive for my pleasure, Emily Richards," said Mr. Redd. "You have such a gorgeous body. One that I would love to see covered in red scars and marks." Mr. Redd placed his hand on Emily's body sensually. His touch was giving Emily chills. "Now that you're mine, I can do with you as I please," he said. "I own your soul. No turning back."

Emily looked scared of Mr. Redd. "You want me to be your sex slave?" she asked. Mr. Redd shook his head.

"No," he said. "I want you to surrender to me willingly." Emily swallowed in fear when she heard Mr. Redd say he wanted her to surrender. She felt terrified. "I did mention there would be rules," Mr. Redd added.

"Rules?" Emily asked. "Are there going to be rules?"

Mr. Redd approached Emily with a sensual gaze in his eyes. "You will attend to my sexual needs as my new submissive," he said.

Emily wasn't sure about this. "And if I don't?" she asked.

Mr. Redd gave her a stern look. "Then I shall have to punish you," he said.

Emily's heart was racing. She wanted to run out of the room, screaming. But she couldn't. Mr. Redd gazed into her eyes as if he were hypnotizing her to make her stay with him. "I'm afraid you can't leave me," he said. "I will bring harm and pain to you and those around you if you refuse me."

He leaned over to kiss her. But Emily stood up in protest. "This wasn't part of the deal," she said.

Mr. Redd smiled at her and gave her a seductive stare. "Oh yes, it is," he said. "You didn't read the fine print on the signed contract." He showed her the contract she had signed the previous night and pointed to a fine print on one of the pages. Emily squinted her eyes closely to read what it said.

"I, Emily Richards, hereafter known as 'the Damned,' offer my immortal soul and my virginity to Mr. Redd as his Submissive for his BDSM pleasure," she said. It made Emily gasp. She looked at Mr. Redd with fear. "I'm your Submissive," she asked.

"Yes, you are," Mr. Redd replied. "You belong to me now. Body and soul forever." Emily had never been submissive to a man before. She read the rest of the agreement in the contract.

"I hereby obey the Dominant's demands without complaints or annoyance at his dominance," she said. "If I dishonor, disobey, or disrespect these terms required by the Dominant, may I forever let my body burn in Hell for all eternity." It wasn't very clear for her to understand. She wanted to tell him "No." But she couldn't.

"I must warn you," Mr. Redd said. "If you say 'No,' I will spank you hard in this room." She had no choice but to agree to be Mr. Redd's slave. She didn't want to upset him.

Mr. Redd returned his shirt and jacket and took her out of his playroom, locking the door behind him afterward. He then brought her into his dining room to have breakfast with him. A few minutes later, Mr. Redd gave Emily a ride back to Halo Town in his helicopter. As they flew through the skies, they headed towards the dawn as the sun rose over the horizon. They landed at the downtown depot, where his limousine was parked outside. They took the elevator down to the lobby and headed out the door. They got into the limo and drove off to Halo University.

Upon arrival, all the students gathered outside the campus. To their surprise, they saw Emily step out of the limo with Mr. Redd holding her in his arms as they walked toward the main entrance. They realized that Emily was no longer the innocent loser or ugly duckling; she was now Mr. Redd's submissive toy. Rumors began to spread all over the campus.

"Everyone is staring," Emily whispered. Mr. Redd grinned as he wrapped his arm around Emily's waist until his hand reached her butt.

"Let them stare," Mr. Redd said to her. He leaned close to her and began to kiss her in front of every student. They all gasped in unison at the sight of Emily kissing Mr. Redd on campus. A few students fainted. Even the three college girls were watching from the window inside the building. They were shocked to see Emily kissing Mr. Redd outside the college.

"Oh my gosh!" said Jetta.

"Emily Richards is in a relationship with Mr. Redd?" Nicole was more than just shocked. She was furious. Her eyes were burning with anger and rage at the sight of Emily in the arms of Mr. Redd. "How dare that ugly duckling?" she said. "Who does she think she is, kissing a man like that?" The college girls left from the window and headed downstairs to the front door.

Meanwhile, the students were still shocked to see the two kissing before them. Mr. Redd's passionate kisses left Emily intoxicated. When he finished, he walked Emily to the main entrance.

"Remember our deal," he said. "I want you to be happy with our relationship." Mr. Redd kissed her again near the front entrance. "I'll see you later," Mr. Redd said as he returned to his limousine. He drove away, and Emily was left blushing. She couldn't tell if it was from embarrassment or pleasure, but she shrugged it off as she entered the college.

After Mr. Redd left, the college students asked her questions about her relationship with Mr. Redd. But Emily told them it was just a simple meeting she had with him. However, the three college girls then came outside to confront Emily. They were the angriest of all.

"I wanna know what you and Mr. Redd were doing," Nicole said.

Emily shook her head in denial. "I don't know what you're talking about," she said. "You must be mistaken."

Suddenly, all the college students asked about her relationship with Mr. Redd. "What was all that kissing you two were doing?" asked Jetta.

"Are you dating?" asked Katie.

But Emily told them it was just a simple meeting she had with him. "He was just dropping me off," she said. "You must be thinking of someone else."

Nicole slapped Emily in the face. She wanted answers about her relationship with Mr. Redd. "**YOU** are in a relationship with him, are you?" Nicole said. "I saw you kissing him on the campus! Are you in a relationship with him?"

Emily pushed Nicole out of her way. "Quit asking me so many questions," she yelled. "I must arrive at class on time." As she tried to make her way through the crowd, Nicole tried to stop her from leaving. She still wanted answers.

"**COME BACK HERE**," Nicole cried. "I'm not done with you, **RICHARDS!!**"

Emily headed inside the building and made her way to class. But as she walked down the hallway, Nicole began to chase her. Emily quickly hid in the girls' bathroom to escape the college girls. She was out of breath, panting. Emily went over to the sink and splashed water on her face. She looked at herself in the mirror. Her cheeks were red with embarrassment. No one has ever asked her these questions.

"Oh my gosh," she said. "I think I need to rest."

A few minutes later, after she calmed down, Emily opened the door slightly and peeked her head out. She checked to see if Nicole was gone. "She's not here," she said. Emily left the bathroom and quickly headed to class.

The next day, Emily woke up in bed. She stretched and yawned before she looked at the clock. It was 8:05 AM and still early. Just then, there was a knock on the door. "Come in," she said.

The door opened wide, and her mother stepped in, carrying a food tray for her. "Breakfast," she said. She set the tray down on Emily's bed. On the tray was a plate of food made specially for her. Emily got the breakfast she wanted: scrambled eggs, hash browns, sausages, and French toast. Next to the plate was a glass of orange juice. Emily was happy to have a real breakfast for a change. Mrs. Richards kissed her on the forehead as she left the bedroom.

Emily started eating breakfast as a distraction from the chase she had encountered the previous day. Just then, the phone rang. Emily got up quickly to answer it.

"Hello," she said. It was Mr. Redd calling her on his cell phone.

"I'm so glad you're there," he said. "How would you like to visit my office?"

Emily took a deep breath before answering his question. "I'll come," she said.

Mr. Redd gave her the time to meet him at his office. "I'll see you when you get here," he said. Emily hung up the phone and finished her plate. After breakfast, she got out of bed and dressed. She went to her closet to find something nice to wear.

A few minutes later, Emily left the house wearing the same red suit Mr. Redd had given her the day before. She took a taxi to Diablo

City instead of Halo University. Upon arriving at Redd Enterprises Inc., Emily exited the cab and headed inside. She made her way to Mr. Redd's office. She saw Mr. Redd standing in a crimson suit and tie at the elevator as she arrived. He smiled at the sight of Emily in her red suit.

"Good morning, Emily," he said.

"Good morning, Mr. Redd," Emily said back. Then, he took her hand and led her to his office down the hallway. But as they walked together, Mr. Redd's eyes were focused on Emily's butt in her tight-fitting skirt. Every sway showcased her curves. It was leaving him feeling turned on. His hand grabbed her butt at first. Then, he spanked her sharply, which made Emily cry a little.

"Ouch!" she said.

As they arrived at his office, Mr. Redd offered her a seat on one end of the table. Then, he began to discuss the terms of their deal. "If you want to maintain your life of luxury, you must follow the fundamental terms I will provide you," he said. Emily understood him. But then, she asked what his fundamental terms and demands were and why she must attend them.

"What are your fundamental terms?" she asked.

Mr. Redd walked around her like a tiger circling its prey. "The fundamental purpose of this contract is to allow the submissive to sell her soul to the dominant for a life of luxury, to explore her sensuality and her limits safely, with due respect and regard for her needs, her limits, and her wellbeing," Mr. Redd said. "All I ask is that you attend to your duties under my command."

Suddenly, he pulled out a crop whip from the sleeve of his blazer jacket and walked around like a military lieutenant giving orders to Army soldiers.

"The contract states that I, the Dominant, offer you, the Submissive, luxury and pleasure," he said. "The submissive shall decide whether to agree or disagree with the following terms. Those terms are to be discussed verbally before being used. Pay attention because this is important." Mr. Redd began to discuss the fundamental terms and service provisions for Emily to follow. Emily sat and listened.

"The submissive accepts the dominant as her master, with the understanding that she is now the property of the dominant, to be dealt with as the dominant pleases during the Terms generally but specifically during the Allotted Times and any additional agreed allotted times," he said. "The submissive shall serve the dominant in any way the dominant sees fit and shall endeavor to please the dominant at all times to the best of her ability. The submissive shall not touch or pleasure herself sexually without permission from the dominant. The submissive shall submit to any sexual activity demanded by the dominant and shall do so without hesitation or argument. The submissive shall address me as 'Sir' or 'Master' in response."

Emily looked at him, confused. She must address Mr. Redd by the title given. "Are there any other titles?" she asked.

"You may also address me as 'Mr. Redd, or 'Devil Daddy,'" he said.

Emily shook her head. "I prefer to call you 'Mr. Redd," she said.

Then, Mr. Redd continued to explain the requirements Emily would receive, which included participation in nightly activities after hours, private sessions in his office, and sexual acts. "The dominant will schedule the time of day for the submissive to be available," he continued. "The submissive shall accept whippings, floggings, spankings, caning, paddling, or any other discipline the dominant should decide to administer without hesitation, inquiry, or complaint. This deal will include specific rules."

But then, Emily stopped him briefly. She knew there was a catch in his deal.

"What are the rules?" she asked.

Mr. Redd faced Emily and explained the rules to her. "The rules state that the submissive must obey any instructions given by the dominant immediately without hesitation or reservation and in an expeditious manner," he said. "She must never abandon him for another. The submissive must never attempt to go beyond the walls of the dominant's home. She must remain within his reach. The submissive will agree to any sexual activity deemed fit and pleasurable by the dominant, except those activities outlined in hard limits. The submissive will not enter into any sexual relations with anyone other than the dominant. The submissive will conduct herself respectfully and modestly at all times. She must recognize that her behavior is a direct reflection of the dominant. The submissive shall be held accountable for any misdeeds, wrongdoings, and misbehavior committed when not in the presence of the dominant. The submissive shall be rewarded if the rules are followed and obeyed properly."

Mr. Redd placed his hand on Emily's chest to illustrate the hard limits for her understanding. Emily gasped at the touch of his hand on her breast.

"Does it turn you on?" he asked.

Emily nodded her head in response.

Mr. Redd squeezed her breast tightly to make her answer his question. "Yes," said Emily.

"That's good," said Mr. Redd. When he removed his hand, he resumed discussing the contract with her. "The dominant shall also address the submissive as 'Princess' for her delight," Mr. Redd continued. "The submissive shall agree to attend events with the dominant, if asked, in a kind yet firm manner."

Emily's eyes widened at his words. She looked up at Mr. Redd and questioned him about what he would do to her. "What happens if I don't follow the rules?" she asked.

Mr. Redd's expression changed. "Failure to comply with any of the rules will result in immediate punishment, the nature of which shall be determined by the dominant," he said. "These involve spanking, flogging, bondage, use of bull whips, paddles, crop whips, and handcuffs." He demonstrated his firm gesture by spanking her bottom with the crop whip. It made Emily let out a shriek from the pain inflicted on her. "Do I make myself clear?" he asked.

Emily whimpered in response to his question. But Mr. Redd spanked her again with a sharper hit. "Yes, Sir," Emily said.

"Good," said Mr. Redd. He returned to his seat and put down the crop whip. "I'm glad you agree with me on these terms," Mr. Redd said.

Emily's butt felt sore from the spanking he gave her. "Don't you think you should ease up on the spankings?" she asked.

Mr. Redd frowned at her for questioning him.

"Why should I?" he said.

Emily rubbed her butt to soften the pain as she told him why he should be gentle with the way he spanked her. "I don't think these are my limits," she said. "Besides, it hurts."

Mr. Redd got up and approached Emily with the crop whip. He pointed it towards her face and lifted her chin to meet his gaze. "Need I remind you of your signed contract?" he asked. Emily remembered the contract and nodded her head in response. "If you ignore these demands, you shall receive your punishment," said Mr. Redd. "Remember that."

Emily stayed with Mr. Redd at his office as his assistant for the rest of the day. She spent the day joining him for business meetings with his executive workers and other chief executive officers from other business companies in Diablo City.

That evening, Mr. Redd and Emily left Redd Enterprises and entered his car. "How was your day at work with me?" Mr. Redd asked.

Emily felt pretty tired. "Who knew a CEO like you would take a day at work so seriously?" she said.

"Welcome to my world," Mr. Redd said. "Now you know how demanding I can be." Then, Mr. Redd took Emily back to Halo Town. When they arrived at Emily's house, Mr. Redd kissed Emily before she got out of the limo. "Try it for a week," he said. "You will learn to enjoy BDSM sex. Trust me."

Emily left the limousine and entered her house. Mr. Redd watched her from a distance and grinned. His eyes changed color for a brief moment before returning to normal. The limo drove away afterward. Emily sat down on the couch and sighed. She began to think about what Mr. Redd said about the terms of BDSM sex and the demands he would give her. She needed more information about BDSM before she made her decision with Mr. Redd when she saw him the next time.

Emily and The Devil

The next day, Emily went onto her laptop and researched BDSM sex on the internet. She came upon a page that explained BDSM sex and what it contained. On the screen, Emily saw pictures of couples dressed in leather holding floggers, bullwhips, and paddles. On another page was a woman strapped to an X-cross, whipped by a man in a leather PVC mask holding a whip in his hand, beating the woman. The image made Emily feel so uncomfortable that she turned off her laptop. After calming down, Emily picked up the phone to call Mr. Redd.

When Mr. Redd answered, Emily began to speak. "I researched BDSM on my laptop," she said.

Mr. Redd was pleased. "That's good," he said. "What did you think of it?"

Emily felt nervous after looking at the pictures. "I think I should hang on to my free will for one week," she said. She hung up the phone and went outside to take a walk.

Later that night, Emily was lying in her room on her bed. Her family was having dinner downstairs in the dining room, but Emily wasn't joining them. Her father was still angry with her when she came home the other day. Suddenly, there was a knock on the door. Emily got out of bed and answered the door.

"I'll get it," she yelled.

When she opened the door, she saw Mr. Redd in the doorway. "Hello, Emily," he said. Emily was surprised to see him at her house. Mr. Redd didn't look happy to see her. His face looked disappointed.

"What are you doing here?" Emily whispered.

"I came to talk with you," Mr. Redd replied.

Emily didn't want Mr. Redd to come in. Her parents were in the dining room, and they could get angry if they saw Mr. Redd in the house. However, Mr. Redd wasn't there to meet Emily's parents. He was there to see Emily alone. "You said you wanted to hang on to your free will," he said.

Emily remembered what she had said to Mr. Redd a week before. "Yes, I said that," she said.

Mr. Redd asked Emily why she said that to him on the phone.

"I figured I'd want our relationship to be simple and romantic without the BDSM stuff," Emily replied.

But Mr. Redd disagreed with Emily's answer. "I told you I don't do romance," he said. "And you can't hold on to your free will because you no longer have any. You are my submissive."

Mr. Redd grabbed Emily's wrist and took her out of her house. He brought her to his limo and put her inside. Then, he got in and told the driver to take them to Diablo City. The limo left Halo Town and returned to Diablo City, arriving at Mr. Redd's penthouse. As they got inside, Mr. Redd took Emily into the living room. Emily sat on the couch, and Mr. Redd stood before her. "I did say punishments would be required if you don't follow the rules," he said. "Or have you forgotten?

Emily looked up at Mr. Redd and trembled. "I'm sorry," she said. "Don't be angry with me."

Mr. Redd grabbed her face with one hand. "You'd better do as I say," he said. "Because I won't be merciful next time." He let go of her and loosened his tie.

"As I mentioned before," Mr. Redd said. "There will be punishments required if you disobey my demands. I could whip you right now if you'd like." Emily shook her head in response. "No, thank you," she said. She was afraid of what punishment he would give her.

"Come," Mr. Redd added. "We must correct the error."

Emily got up from the couch and followed Mr. Redd down the hallway. They headed into the playroom, where Mr. Redd gave Emily his instructions. "First, I want you to get on your knees," he said. He pointed her to a bed with bondage poles. At the end of the floor was a shag rug with a black star. Emily wasn't the reason she needed to be on her knees. Mr. Redd frowned. "I said get on your knees," he said. So Emily walked over to the bed and got on her knees. Mr. Redd approached her and demanded that she face him. Next, he unzipped his pants in front of Emily. "Now, I want you to suck on this," said Mr. Redd. He pulled out his manhood and allowed Emily to give him a blowjob.

Emily looked at him oddly. "You want me to do what?" she asked.

Mr. Redd frowned. "Do you want to keep your life of luxury?" he asked.

"Yes," Emily replied.

"Then, suck my cock," Mr. Redd demanded. "Suck it good and hard. If you do a good job, I will reward you. If not, I will punish you."

Emily had no choice. She closed her eyes and opened her mouth. Mr. Redd smacked her face slightly. "Don't close your eyes," he said. "I want to look into your eyes while you suck me."

Emily opened her eyes and began to give Mr. Redd a blowjob in the playroom. Mr. Redd inserted his cock inside Emily's mouth slowly. His size was so massive that the thickness of his manhood stretched Emily's mouth. Mr. Redd moaned as Emily took him inside her mouth. He thrusted his hips towards her face, hitting her throat with force. Emily felt every hit he was giving her. She thought she would be sick, but Emily didn't stop because she didn't want Mr. Redd to punish her. So Emily continued sucking his cock. As she did, Mr. Redd moaned louder. He gritted his teeth and groaned as he thrusted harder while his gaze locked on Emily's eyes. His eyes filled with hunger for lustful need. The pleasure was building inside him to the point he threw his head back in orgasm. He released a massive load inside Emily's mouth as he let out a roar.

He pulled his cock out of Emily's mouth and brought her up to him.

"You did an excellent job," he said. "For that, I shall reward you." Mr. Redd removed his shirt and pants and began to undress her. His hands gripped her butt sharply, which made Emily let out a cry of pain. He continued to touch and kiss Emily before removing her bra and panties. His touch completely warmed Emily. She could feel herself getting horny from how he was groping her breasts. Mr. Redd's lips left a trail of kisses all over her neck. Then, he bit her neck sharply. Emily cried in pain from his sharp teeth. Mr. Redd unhooked her bra and slid the straps off her shoulders. He tossed the bra aside before returning his attention to her bare breasts. They were not small. However, it was a natural 42D cup size. Her nipples were perky from the sudden cold air. Mr. Redd purred with delight at seeing her body, just as it had been before, in his bedroom. Emily opened her eyes and found herself topless. But Mr. Redd stopped her from covering herself.

"No need to hide your body from me," he said. "You are sexy. Flaunt it." He removed her panties afterward and tossed them away, leaving her completely naked from head to toe.

Mr. Redd turned Emily around and bent her over onto the bed. He opened her legs wide and inserted his right hand inside her womanly parts. His long fingers circled her clitoris as he cupped her breast with his left hand. Emily moaned in pleasure, feeling Mr. Redd's hands all over her body. Her breath quickened, and she moaned louder. Mr. Redd removed his hand from her clitoris and inserted his cock inside her vaginal opening. Emily gasped when she felt his massive manhood enter from behind.

"Does that feel good?" Mr. Redd asked.

Emily moaned at first. But then, Mr. Redd squeezed her breast tightly to get her to answer his question. "Yes," Emily said. Mr. Redd softened his grip as he began to penetrate her.

He grabbed Emily's hips and thrusted deep inside her. Mr. Redd's moans mixed with Emily's moans within the walls of the playroom. Finally, they orgasmed at the same time. Mr. Redd removed his cock from Emily and lay her down on the bed. Emily was breathless from her orgasm. Mr. Redd leaned in towards her and looked into her eyes. "That wasn't so bad," he said. "Did you enjoy it?"

Emily looked at Mr. Redd and smiled. "I did," she said. Mr. Redd smiled back. He was pleased to see Emily looking satisfied.

Emily trembled at the sound of Mr. Redd's words. But then, he took her to the whipping bench. He secured her hands and feet with leather cuffs on the bench. Mr. Redd pulled out a leather whip and began to whip her body with force. Emily whimpered in panic. She cried out in pain. But it only made him whip her some more.

"I can do this all night if you want me to," he said softly. He continued whipping her even harder. The sounds echoed sharply in the room, merging with Emily's cries. Then, he stopped and began to kiss her again. His hot lips muffled her noises. He uncuffed her and began to remove his man briefs, exposing his massive manhood. Now, he, too, was naked. He positioned himself on top of her just like before and began to have sex with her in his playroom. Every thrust he made caused Emily to scream. Mr. Redd grunted and groaned with pleasure as he penetrated more deeply and more complexly inside her. The pleasure was building up inside. Emily cried some more as she felt his hot flesh slam against her skin like the whip he gave her. Until, at last, Mr. Redd exploded in orgasm.

When it was over, he got up off of Emily and put his pants back on. He saw Emily's body covered in red marks. However, she was fortunate to be still alive. Mr. Redd took her in his arms and touched her face.

"I can feel you are in pain," he whispered. "But I find solace in being here for you. Your vulnerability is a testament to the depth of our connection, and it moves me in ways I cannot fully express."

Then, he took her out of the playroom and brought her to his bedroom, locking the playroom door behind him. In his bedroom, Mr. Redd handed her a red nightgown to wear to bed. The two kissed before Emily fainted onto his bed in exhaustion. Mr. Redd smiled as he saw Emily's body lying on the satin sheets of his bed. Mr. Redd wanted another round with her. He placed his hands on her and leaned in close to her face. His tongue licked her whip marks before he began his second time having sex with Emily.

He positioned himself on top of her again and began to thrust his manhood inside her for the second time. He got hard again as he penetrated her on his bed. It made him moan loudly with pleasure as he thrusted his hips harder and faster. He licked her breast with his tongue while he penetrated her. Emily moaned in her sleep as Mr. Redd continued thrusting inside her on his bed. The more he thrusted her, the more aroused he became. Every sensation was leaving him shaking all over. Finally, he released a second orgasm. Mr. Redd was exhausted from his second time of sex with Emily in his bed. But he was pleased. After that, he was satisfied with his orgasm. Emily went to sleep in Mr. Redd's bed. While she slept, Mr. Redd watched her from the comfort of his chair.

"Soon, you will see things my way," he said in a low, deep voice.

# Chapter 7

The next day, Emily awoke to the sound of a piano playing. She got out of bed and made her way into the living room. There, she saw Mr. Redd playing an aria from the opera, "Faust." Mr. Redd saw Emily and smiled.

"Good morning," he said. "It's so lovely of you to walk in."

Emily was still aching from the pain she had had last night. "Mr. Redd," she said. "As you mentioned last night, I want to say..." But before she could finish, Mr. Redd interrupted her. He got up off the piano bench and gave Emily a present. Inside was a diamond necklace for her to wear. The diamonds were real, not fake, like costume jewelry.

"Where did you get this?" Emily asked.

Mr. Redd smiled when he answered her question. "I saw it in a window display and bought it for you," he said. "I want you to wear it." Emily looked at the necklace and was speechless. "Would you like to try it on?" Mr. Redd asked.

Emily nodded her head in response. He put the necklace around Emily's neck, and she looked in the mirror. She looked like a full-grown woman wearing diamonds. Mr. Redd came up behind her.

"You are my Belle of the Ball," he said. He wrapped his arms around her and began touching her seductively. "I want to see you wearing this every day," he whispered.

Emily escaped from his embrace and looked away from the mirror for a brief minute. Then, she looked at Mr. Redd. "Listen, Mr. Redd," said Emily in a serious tone. "I want to discuss what we did last night." Mr. Redd thought she was going to say she didn't like it. But he shrugged off the thought and allowed Emily to speak.

"What did you want to discuss with me?" he asked.

Emily told him that they could talk in his office. So, Mr. Redd and Emily went down the hallway and entered his private office to discuss the terms of their previous night in the playroom. Mr. Redd sat down at his desk and pulled the contract out of his drawer. "Take a seat," he said.

Emily sat down in a chair and began to share what she liked and disliked about it. "I'm okay with the touching and kissing," she said. "But I'm not okay with bondage rope or the use of handcuffs or the spankings during sex."

Mr. Redd felt disappointed at first, but respected Emily's opinion. "I understand," he said. "Please continue."

Next, Emily told Mr. Redd what she would do and what she would not do in the playroom. "No nipple clamps, paddles, or hot wax," she said. "I don't want to be hit with a cane or anything painful."

Mr. Redd nodded his head. "Understood," he responded. Emily also mentioned that she could do blindfolding, but didn't want to do bondage with tape or butt plugs. "Consider them gone," said Mr.

Redd. Then, Mr. Redd explains the remaining items that he will use on Emily. "There will be the use of leather cuffs," he said. "Blindfolds and lingerie are optional. You will wear them for my pleasure." Emily stopped him for a second to ask a question. "This all sounds tempting," she said. "But shouldn't I get a safeword?"

Mr. Redd looked at Emily with a fiery stare. "What?" he asked.

Emily cleared her throat before she could speak. "Most BDSM dominants would give their submissives safewords if things become too rough for them," she said.

Mr. Redd groaned with annoyance and slicked back his hair. "You want me to give you a safeword?" he asked.

Emily replied, "Yes." She wanted to ensure she would have a safeword to protect her safety.

Mr. Redd sighed. "Very well," he said. Then, he began to explain about the safeword Emily would be given. "The submissive is to receive a safe word to use in such circumstances related to this," he said. "The safeword will be invoked depending on the severity of the demands."

Emily thought for a minute before she asked her question. "What is the safeword for me to use?" she asked.

"The safeword is 'Freedom,'" said Mr. Redd. "It will bring to the attention of the dominant that the submissive cannot tolerate any further demands. When this word is spoken, the dominant's action will cease completely, effective immediately, and the submissive is free."

Emily understood the concept of being given a safeword to use. "If I use my safeword, everything you do to me will stop?" she asked.

Mr. Redd groaned in response. "Precisely," he said. She was unaware that Mr. Redd intended to make sure Emily wouldn't use her safeword anytime soon.

Emily looked at Mr. Redd and cleared her throat. "Promise you will be less aggressive next time," she said.

"I promise to be less aggressive next time," replied Mr. Redd. "If you promise to trust me."

Emily smiled at Mr. Redd's promise. "I trust you," she said.

"If things get too rough with you," said Mr. Redd. "Use your safeword, and I will stop." Emily agreed and began to leave his office. Soon, they left the penthouse and headed outside. Emily got into the Ford Mustang with Mr. Redd, and they drove off.

A few minutes later, Emily arrived home and exited Mr. Redd's Ford Mustang. "Remember, Emily," said Mr. Redd. "Next time we go to my playroom, your expectations will be rewarded."

Emily smiled. "Thank you," she said. Mr. Redd watched her from behind and became aroused at the sight of her butt in the tight-fitting skirt. He imagined penetrating her from behind in his playroom with her body strapped to the whipping bench, naked, with her butt exposed. Mr. Redd thought he could keep Emily for himself. He wasn't going to let her out of his sight. He grinned wickedly, knowing that he would keep her with him as long as she didn't use her safe word. He closed the door as Emily entered the house and drove off. He couldn't wait until he went on another date with Emily the next time.

Later that afternoon, Emily was at home, sitting on the couch in the living room. As she was lying on the couch, her parents came into the room with some questions to ask her.

"Where have you been?" Mr. Richards asked. "We were worried about you, Emily."

Emily sat up and looked at her parents. They were upset with her. "What's the matter?" she asked. Her parents began to badger her about her date with Mr. Redd the night before.

"Did you do anything with Mr. Redd?" Mrs. Richards asked.

"What did he do to you?" Mr. Richards asked. "Did you sleep with him? Did he touch you in any way?"

Emily didn't want to answer them. It was similar to this morning at college when Nicole asked her in the hallway. So she said, "We didn't do anything." It made her parents furious. Mr. Richards slapped Emily in the face the second time. He wanted an answer from her about Mr. Redd.

"Emily, I want an answer," he yelled. "What did Mr. Redd do to you? Answer me!!" Emily was shocked to hear how angry her Father sounded. She got up from the couch and went upstairs to her room. Mr. Richards tried to stop her, but she slammed the door in his face. He knocked on the door loudly. "**EMILY ABIGAIL RICHARDS,**" he shouted. "**OPEN THIS DOOR!!**"

Emily covered her ears to block out the noise. "**GO AWAY!**" she yelled. Mr. Richards was upset with his daughter's stubbornness. So he went back downstairs to watch TV in the living room with her Father gone. Emily lay down on her bed in her room. She was relaxing both her body and mind. Looking up at the ceiling, Emily could hear her Father's voice asking her questions about Mr. Redd.

That evening, Emily took a shower to clear her mind of the night she had spent with Mr. Redd. After she got out of the shower, she dried herself with a towel. She walked over to the mirror and looked at her reflection. Just then, there was a knock on the door. Marcus pounded on the door, telling Emily he needed to use the bathroom. So Emily left the bathroom with the towel around her body and entered her bedroom. Emily heard a knock on the door. "Come in," she said.

Her mother came into the room. "How was your date with Mr. Redd last night?" she asked.

Emily wanted to tell her, but remembered what Mr. Redd said. She wasn't going to tell anyone about what happened between the two of them. Especially after her first night of sex with him. So she just smiled and said, "It was okay."

Mrs. Richards smiled. "That's nice," she said. But then, she noticed the red marks on her body. "Where did you get those marks?" she asked. Emily told her it was just a sunburn.

Mrs. Richards gave her a questionable look. "Are you sure?" she asked.

Emily looked nervous, but she quickly responded, "Yes, I'm sure."

Emily exhaled. She didn't want her mother to worry. But as Emily was about to rest, she began to ask her Mom a question. "Has Dad calmed down yet?" she asked.

Mrs. Richards told Emily she was worried about her and wanted to know what had happened with her and Mr. Redd. Emily didn't have an answer. She was more frightened by how her Father threatened her in the living room. Mrs. Richards left her bedroom and went to the kitchen to cook dinner. Emily didn't feel like eating dinner with her family. So she went to bed to forget about her Father's voice.

The next day, Emily arrived at Halo University. However, she saw a crowd of students waiting for her as she came. They had many questions to ask her about her relationship with Mr. Redd. The rumors had reached every student body on campus. Emily didn't want to be asked by so many people.

"Please," she said. "Excuse me. Let me through." So she went inside the building. But as she was walking down the hallway, the three college girls appeared. This time, they were furious with Emily's newfound popularity.

"**Emily, you little bitch**," Nicole shouted. "What did Mr. Redd do to you? Did you sleep with him? Did you get laid with him? Did he have sex with you?"

Emily was starting to panic. "I don't know what you're talking about," she said.

"I'm talking about your so-called newfound confidence," Nicole yelled. "I want answers! Did you or did you **NOT** have sex with him?"

Jetta and Katie approached her in anger. "Better speak now or forever hold your peace," said Jetta.

"What were you and Mr. Redd doing together?" asked Katie. "Well?"

Emily didn't want to answer her questions. "Please, stop," she said. "I don't have time for questions." However, Nicole didn't want her to leave until she forced her to answer her questions. The more Nicole pushed her to answer her, the more frightened Emily became. Sweat began to form on Emily's forehead. Her heartbeat quickened.

"What were you doing with him?" Nicole asked. "**WELL**? I'm waiting." She kept questioning her repeatedly.

Emily stepped back in fear. "Stop it, Nicole," she said. "You're scaring me."

Nicole kept asking as she came closer to her, becoming more furious. "I want to know what you and Mr. Redd did," she said. Emily continued to back away until Nicole exploded, "**ANSWER ME!!!!**" Emily felt threatened when Nicole yelled at her. She slapped Nicole in her face without warning. "**SMACK!**"

Jetta and Katie gasped. Emily looked at Nicole, who had fallen onto the floor with a red mark on her face. "I'm sorry," she said. But Nicole didn't forgive her. She got up off the floor and began to fight Emily.

"You're dead, Richards," she roared. All the students came in and saw the fight happening in the hallway. Nicole came at Emily, slapping her face and kicking at her.

All the students chanted. "Fight! Fight! Fight!"

Emily didn't want to fight Nicole. She tried to escape, but Jetta and Katie held her still for Nicole to strike back. "I will send you straight to Hell, you fucking whore," Nicole growled. She was about to punch Emily in the face, sending her crashing to the floor.

Suddenly, Dean Woodrow, the Dean of Halo University, stopped the fighting between the two women. "Is this any way to behave in our prestigious halls?" he said.

Nicole got up and told the Dean about Emily's relationship with Mr. Redd. "She should be removed permanently from Halo University," she said. "She's a whore!"

Emily and The Devil

All the students gasped at hearing Nicole address Emily as a whore. Nicole began to tell everyone about Emily in a negative manner. "She slept with Mr. Redd in his penthouse," she said. "She's a whore! Emily Richards is guilty of adultery!"

Dean Woodrow got angry. He took Nicole by her arm and pulled her away. "That's enough from you," Dean Woodrow said. He took Nicole to his office. Jetta and Katie joined her. Emily turned around to look at the students looking at her. She thought they would be mad at her for attacking Nicole. But they weren't. It was the first time Emily stood up for herself. She received praise from her peers for her courage in standing up to Nicole. It made her feel special.

Later that afternoon, Emily came home from another day at college. She was carrying a bag of new clothes and shoes she had bought with the money she received from Mr. Redd. She went upstairs to try on her new clothes as she got inside. Her parents weren't at home. They were going to a basketball game with Marcus. She went into her bedroom to try on her evening dresses. She looked mature and sophisticated in each of the dresses she tried on. Some were loose-fitting, while the others were tight-fitting. As she saw herself in the mirror, she remembered what Nicole called her in the hallway in front of everyone. "A whore!" Emily made a face. Then, a thought occurred to her. "If Nicole thinks I'm a whore," she thought. "Then, she's wrong." She went over to her phone and called Mr. Redd.

"Hello," she said. "I want to speak with Mr. Redd, please."

Just then, she heard Mr. Redd's voice on the other end of the line. "Hello, Emily," he said. "I was just about to call you, but I knew you would call me. I had just stepped out of the shower." Emily was surprised to hear that Mr. Redd was aware of her call. "How would you like to join me for dinner tonight?" Mr. Redd asked. Emily inquired about the location of their meeting. "In my office," Mr. Redd replied. "I'll see you at 7:00 pm." Then, Emily told him she would wear a tight-fitting dress for him. It made Mr. Redd twitch with delight. She hung up the phone and resumed her search for an outfit.

That evening at 6:54 pm, Emily left the house wearing a tight-fitting pink cocktail dress. She returned to Redd Enterprises Inc. in Diablo City to meet Mr. Redd in his office. Emily stepped out of the elevator and headed to his office. When she came in, Mr. Redd was waiting for her. His eyes widened at the sight of Emily in a tight-fitting dress. It suited her.

"That is one hell of a dress," he said. His eyes focused on her curves. Her hips, breasts, and legs were noticeable under the fabric. He purred with delight. He invited her inside and offered her a seat at a table made for two. There were candles surrounding the place. It was a romantic setting. Perfect for two people to have dinner.

"I've never seen your office like this," said Emily.

"I knew you would find it alluring," Mr. Redd said. Then, he offered her a seat on one end of the table as he took his seat on the other. As Emily sat down, Mr. Redd noticed her breasts jiggling slightly. His eyes gleamed at the sight of her breasts. He began to imagine putting his hands and his mouth on them. "You are such a tease," he said.

Emily blushed. "Please, Mr. Redd," she said. "This is just for tonight." Mr. Redd agreed. He continued to be a gentleman. He wanted to make Emily feel comfortable tonight.

"What's on your mind?" Mr. Redd asked.

Emily placed her hands on the table and began to speak. "It's about Nicole," she said.

Mr. Redd gave Emily a look. "What about her?" he asked.

Emily explained to him what Nicole had said to her at college today. "She called me a whore," she said. "Nicole asked me questions about our relationship. But then, she attacked me. So I slapped her in the face."

Mr. Redd laughed about what Emily had done to Nicole, but then returned to his casual manner. "So Nicole called you a whore?" he asked.

"Yes," Emily responded. "But I'm not a whore."

Suddenly, Mr. Redd's expression changed. His eyes turned blood red with temptation and seduction. His smile curled his lip as he leaned in closer to his seat. He looked into Emily's eyes and arched his eyebrow.

"You are a whore," said Mr. Redd.

Emily looked at him, confused. "What do you mean?" she asked.

Mr. Redd raised his hand and pointed at Emily's pink dress. His finger traced an outline of her body mid-air as his gaze locked onto Emily's face. "You are *my* whore," he said. "One I could play with seductively."

Emily cleared her throat and covered her mouth with her napkin, embarrassed by Mr. Redd's words. "No, I'm not," she said.

However, Mr. Redd's eyes glowed briefly, drawing Emily's gaze to him. "Yes, you are," he said. "When you go to college the next day, you will show Nicole how much of a whore you are."

Emily felt hypnotized by Mr. Redd's words like a moth to a flame. Just then, two beautiful women entered the office, bearing food for Mr. Redd and Emily on silver trays—grilled fish with pasta and salad for dinner. Emily was amazed at the sight of her plate.

"It looks incredible," she said. Mr. Redd offered Emily some wine. "Thank you," she said. Mr. Redd sat there and watched Emily eat. He took a first bite of his dinner and watched Emily sip wine from the glass. A hiccup escaped her mouth, just as it had before at the fancy restaurant in Halo Town.

"Isn't it wonderful?" Mr. Redd asked. "A lovely dinner with the most beautiful woman in the world."

Emily felt lightheaded after drinking the wine. She could barely stay focused. "I have to leave now," she said in a slightly slurred voice. "My parents will be wondering where I am."

Mr. Redd stopped her for a minute. "You say you're leaving," he said. "But your body tells you to stay."

Emily looked at him with confusion. "What do you mean?" she asked.

Mr. Redd observed her body as he looked at her with seduction in his eyes. "Your eyes gleam so brightly at the sight of my face," he said. "The way you press your thighs together, and your cheeks turn pink with desire, the changing of your breathing, and the heaving of your chest beneath that top. Your breasts are begging to be free to be touched by my hand."

Emily shook her head in disbelief. "Maybe it's the wine," she said.

"It's not the wine," Mr. Redd said. "It's the adrenaline."

Emily noticed his hand reaching out towards her. She gasped as he placed his hand on her left breast lightly. "Don't be afraid," Mr. Redd said. "It's just a touch. You look so gorgeous under candlelight."

Emily's heart was beating again. She tried to look away, but she couldn't resist the gorgeous look on Mr. Redd's face. He looked like a movie star in a restaurant scene. His eyes mirrored the tender flicker of the candles, casting a romantic glow that danced across his features. His subtle yet alluring smile seemed to promise secrets and sweet nothings. With a physique sculpted like a deity, every movement he made was imbued with an effortless grace, making him the embodiment of romance.

"Your heart is beating," he said. Emily tried to sober herself up to stop the beating. But she failed. "I've never heard such a lovely rhythm," Mr. Redd said. "It's almost as if I could dance to the beat. Like a drum playing music inside your beautiful, luscious chest."

Emily's face turned crimson. The sound of his voice tingled her ears like a melody. She was feeling faint. She surrendered to his embrace, seeking the comfort of a baby in his arms. But she didn't.

After they finished, Mr. Redd called his servants to take the plates away. Emily looked at his servants. Then, she looked at Mr. Redd. "You must go through many contracts with these women," she said.

Mr. Redd scoffed. "They're just my employees," he replied. "I only tell them to do a good job. It's how I whip them into shape." Hearing his remark, Emily laughed a little. Mr. Redd stared at her. "You are a tease," he said. "Even the sound of your laughter is beautiful." He got up from his seat and walked towards Emily. He kissed her as his hands reached around and grabbed her buttocks. His deep kisses left Emily moaning in pleasure. "I would like to have you for dessert," Mr. Redd whispered. Emily gasped as he spanked her hard. They returned to the penthouse as they had before.

Mr. Redd led her inside and offered her a seat in the living room. Emily thanked Mr. Redd for a wonderful dinner. "Anything for you, my dear Emily," Mr. Redd said. "But the night is not over yet."

Emily blushed. She was being spoiled rotten by how Mr. Redd was treating her. "I have a special treat for us," he said. Emily sat down gracefully as Mr. Redd offered her a glass of wine. He sat down at the piano and played a little tune for her.

Emily was amazed at his piano skills. "I didn't know you played," she said.

Mr. Redd looked up at her face. "I've been playing for years," he said. Emily's eyes grew wide. The music he was playing for her was so beautiful. It was almost hypnotic. His melody drew Emily in. The tune caressed her ears as every key hit her in hidden places. It left Emily throwing her head back in arousal. It was like sex to her.

She writhed in pleasure, hearing Mr. Redd play. The music was seducing her. He stopped playing the piano for a bit and came over to Emily. "How do you feel?" he asked.

Emily moaned again. "I feel so undone," she said in a sexy, breathy voice. Mr. Redd smiled. He took her face in his hands and kissed her. Then, he placed his hand on her right breast and squeezed it. Emily gasped. His touch was electrifying. She could no longer contain herself. She wanted him. She wanted him badly. She placed her hand on his face and pulled him towards her. The two of them kissed on the couch.

They got up off the couch and went straight to the playroom. Mr. Redd handed Emily a black mini-dress with leather cuffs. Emily looked at the items and gave Mr. Redd a quizzical expression.

"What's this?" she asked.

"I want you to wear that dress and those cuffs," Mr. Redd said. "I want to see you like this when I enter the playroom." Emily was confused. Mr. Redd wanted her to wear a black mini-dress and handcuffs on her wrists for him.

"Why do you want me to wear this stuff?" she asked.

"So I could play with you, my submissive toy," Mr. Redd replied. "Take off that pink dress and put on the black dress for me." Emily obeyed his orders by removing her pink, tight-fitting dress and wearing her black mini-dress. However, Mr. Redd added that Emily must take off her bra and panties while wearing the clothing he gave her. So she did. She slid off her white panties and bra, laying them beside her pink dress on the floor. Mr. Redd took her hand and guided her to the foot of the bed.

"Get on your knees," he demanded. Emily obeyed him by getting down on her knees. Then, Mr. Redd told her to face him and look him in the eyes. He put the handcuffs on her wrists and laid them on her thighs. "This is how I want to see you," he said.

Emily felt awkward wearing a mini-dress and kneeling for a man. Then, Mr. Redd walked off briefly to change into something more comfortable. A few minutes later, he returned, wearing black leather pants and no shirt. His chest was bare and oiled. He was holding a crop whip in his hand. Snapping the whip, he glared at Emily. "You've been a very naughty girl, have you?" he asked. Emily shook in fear at the sight of Mr. Redd armed with a crop whip.

Emily shook her head when she looked at her dress. "Is this dress necessary?" she asked.

Mr. Redd positioned his whip towards her face. "Oh yes, it is," he answered. The dress he gave her was too revealing and too provocative. But Mr. Redd was particularly fond of her in lingerie. He went around her and began to whip her back with the crop whip. Then, he lowered it to her buttocks. With a sharp whip, Emily let out a cry. Mr. Redd grabbed her by her neck and pulled her back. "Don't scream," he said. "I want you to accept this as your pleasure for me." He continued whipping her before putting down the crop whip. He lifted Emily to meet his gaze.

They began to kiss again. Then, Mr. Redd took her to a wall lined with red leather and chains. He took her handcuffed wrists and secured them on the wall. They began to have sex again, using the sex items in the playroom. Mr. Redd used crop whips on Emily for his enjoyment and pleasure. He suspended her from the ceiling with leather straps and penetrated her from both the front and back. Mr. Redd was leaving Emily writhing in pleasure and pain. He gave her oral and anal sex in various positions until it was over. Emily was covered entirely in male ejaculation and red marks on her body. Her hair was a tangled mess. Mr. Redd enjoyed it all. He was exhausted from his orgasm. "You see, Emily?" he said in a breathy voice. "You *ARE* a whore." They left the playroom and returned to his bedroom.

The next day, Emily woke up feeling refreshed. She looked out the window at the city view below. The sun was shining, and Emily could hear the distant sound of car horns. Mr. Redd came into the room wearing a t-shirt and sweatpants.

"Good morning," he said. "I'm so glad to see you're awake." Emily got out of bed and put on a silk bathrobe. "Does it feel good to wake up in a luxurious bed?" Mr. Redd asked.

Emily stretched and yawned. "It sure does," she said. "I feel great." Mr. Redd smiled. Then, she joined Mr. Redd in the kitchen to have breakfast. Afterward, Mr. Redd dressed in his business suit, while Emily got dressed in her red suit, complete with a tight-fitting skirt. Emily and Mr. Redd left the penthouse and returned to Halo Town in his black Ford Mustang instead of his limo. Driving down the road, Mr. Redd turned on some music for Emily.

They arrived at Halo University ten minutes later. When Emily got out, she said "goodbye" to Mr. Redd before walking away. As Mr. Redd drove off, Emily made her way inside the building. After yesterday's quarrel with Nicole, all the students waited for her in the hallway. Emily was surprised to see a crowd of students waiting for her. She wondered if they were there to congratulate her for standing up to Nicole or if they could be an angry mob out to get her. Emily didn't know. So she went inside the building on her way to class.

Walking down the hallway, Emily could see pictures of herself in the naughty black mini-dress outfit and handcuffs on every wall. "Where did those pictures come from?" she asked. Emily tried to remove them from the walls before anyone saw them. Suddenly, she heard Dean Woodrow's voice on the intercom. Dean Woodrow called Emily to his office to discuss the fight with Nicole. Emily headed to the Dean's office alone. When she arrived, Emily could see Dean Woodrow sitting at his desk. He gave her a displeasing look and told Emily to sit in a chair.

"Miss Richards," Dean Woodrow said. "Your altercation with Nicole yesterday is strictly prohibited in our prestigious halls at Halo University. I will not tolerate this kind of behavior." Emily remembered her fight yesterday and apologized for her actions.

"I promise," she said. "It won't happen again." Dean Woodrow frowned at Emily. He stood up from his desk and pulled out a piece of paper. But it was a picture of Emily in a mini-dress. He showed it to Emily as he explained the picture. "I found this on the walls this morning," he said. "I will not tolerate your indecent display on campus. I will let you off with a warning, Miss Richards. However, if you engage in such behavior again, you will be expelled from Halo University. Do I make myself clear?"

Emily lowered her head. "Yes, Sir," she answered.

Emily and The Devil

Dean Woodrow let Emily leave his office and go to class. "I'll be keeping an eye on you," he said.

That evening, when Emily came home, she found a package on the floor addressed to her. The package was from Mr. Redd, wrapped in red paper with black ribbons. Emily wanted to know who sent it. She picked up the package and read the card attached to the front. On the card was Mr. Redd's name written in red ink. Emily opened the package and found some lingerie and a pair of red stiletto heels inside. Emily read a note in red ink. "Wear this outfit to college," she read. "Show those doubters who you truly are as my submissive." Emily's eyes popped open at the note's contents.

"I can't wear this to college," she said. But then, she read the rest of the note on the back. "If you refuse my demands," she read. "I will have to discipline you severely." Emily had never heard anything aggressive coming from Mr. Redd. So she agreed to wear the outfit. Looking in the mirror, she could see that Mr. Redd had only given her a naughty schoolgirl uniform for bedroom role-playing, not for college attire. Emily wanted to remove the outfit and wear her regular clothes. But then, the telephone rang. Emily answered it.

"Hello," she said.

"Are you wearing the sexy outfit I bought you?" Mr. Redd said on the phone.

Emily sighed with annoyance. "Yes, I am," she said.

"Good," Mr. Redd replied. "Now, come to my playroom tonight."

Emily gasped. Mr. Redd wanted her to come to his playroom wearing the outfit. It initially made Emily shake with fear. "I can't," she said. "I don't want anyone to see me in this outfit."

Mr. Redd growled on the phone, demanding that Emily come to his penthouse dressed like a schoolgirl. So Emily agreed to Mr. Redd's demands. She wore the naughty college outfit and left her house, wearing a long trench coat to hide her outfit from the public. Emily returned to Mr. Redd's penthouse alone in a taxi. She felt embarrassed about wearing the outfit Mr. Redd had given her.

When Emily arrived, she met Mr. Redd in the playroom. He was wearing a leather jacket and pants with no shirt. Mr. Redd welcomed Emily to his playroom with a smile. "There's my naughty little student," he said. Emily's cheeks turned red with embarrassment. She removed her coat to show Mr. Redd her schoolgirl outfit. Mr. Redd's eyes grew wide. He admired Emily in a naughty outfit he bought her. He witnessed the sight of her breasts in the tight blouse, the hourglass figure in the middle displaying her belly, and her legs in thigh-high stockings matching the mini-skirt, which barely covered the lower half of her body. Mr. Redd brought Emily to the bondage bed and bent her over. "You just earned yourself detention," he said. Mr. Redd pretended to be Emily's teacher and pulled out a ruler. With a sharp hit, Mr. Redd smacked Emily's butt.

Next, Mr. Redd showed Emily some items on the shelves to the right. They were sex toys he bought from adult stores Downtown. He bought spanking paddles and bondage ropes.

"What are those for?" Emily asked.

Mr. Redd seductively raised an eyebrow at her. "You'll see, my little submissive," he responded. Mr. Redd stripped Emily of her clothes until she was completely naked. Then, he took her to the bondage bed. Mr. Redd tied her hands and feet to the bed with a red rope. "Just relax," he said. "You have nothing to fear. I'm going to make you enjoy it."

Mr. Redd put a blindfold over Emily's eyes so she wouldn't see what he was going to do to her. Then, Mr. Redd picked up a feather and lightly caressed her body with it, over her thighs and up to her breasts. Emily whimpered and moaned. The touch was sending her chills. Then, Mr. Redd brought out a leather bullwhip and began to whip her body vigorously. Emily cried. Mr. Redd whipped her some more. Then, he stopped.

Mr. Redd pulled Emily's hair and brought her face to him. "Who's your master?" he asked.

Emily was still in tears. But she answered his question. "You are, Mr. Redd," she said.

Mr. Redd smirked. "Exactly," he said. "Don't forget it."

He let go of her hair and undressed himself in front of her. He straddled her naked body and began to have sex with her again. Mr.

Redd looked at Emily and growled. He penetrated her multiple times until they reached an orgasm in the playroom. After it was over, Mr. Redd untied her from her rope bonds and kissed her on the lips.

He brought her out of the playroom and into the bedroom. Emily lay down on the bed naked. Mr. Redd admired Emily's body. His gaze traced every inch of her curves, covered in red scars and marks. Little drops of blood seeped from the wounds onto the sheets. However, the sheets were red, making it difficult to detect the blood. Mr. Redd lay down next to Emily and wrapped his arm around her.

"Sleep, my submissive," he whispered. "Come sunrise, you will bring me more of your body." He growled in Emily's ear, sending shivers down her spine. Her skin pearled with goosebumps from the sensation of Mr. Redd's breath like cold air on a winter day.

# Chapter 8

One week later, Emily was home with her parents on a Saturday. However, they didn't appear to be happy with her. They were feeling concerned for Emily and her relationship with Mr. Redd. Emily's relationship worried her parents because she was never at home every night. They feared losing their daughter to a man like Mr. Redd.

"What's the matter?" she asked.

"It's about Mr. Redd," said Mr. Richards. "You should stop going out with him."

Emily wasn't sure what they meant by not seeing Mr. Redd anymore. "We're worried about you," Mrs. Richards said. They were worried for Emily's sake and might risk losing her to Mr. Redd. They feared that if she continued her romantic, sexual relationship with Mr. Redd, she would get hurt. But Emily didn't believe them.

"You're wrong," she said. "Mr. Redd is a gentleman. You're just jealous because you never gave me a life of luxury like he did."

"Well, that's just it," Mrs. Richards said. "It's this luxurious lifestyle he's been providing for you. It would help if you didn't have that anymore. This Mr. Redd character is a criminal." But Emily didn't think he was a criminal. Mr. Redd offered Emily a luxurious life, proving to them that he was not a bad person. But Emily's parents were still concerned.

"Emily, be reasonable," Mrs. Richards said. "We just want you to stay away from him." Emily still didn't want to listen to them. She thought they were crazy.

"As long as you're with Mr. Redd, you are in danger," said Mr. Richards.

Emily needed clarification. "Danger?" she said. "What do you mean by danger?"

Mr. Richards explained to Emily that he had noticed the red marks on her body, which her mother had observed a few days prior. "Did Mr. Redd hurt you in any way?" he asked.

Emily was shocked to be asked a serious question by her father about Mr. Redd. "He did whip me and spanked me more than once," she said. "I was given a safe word if the actions became too much for me."

Both her parents gasped. "Emily, that man is a sadist," said Mrs. Richards. "He's using you for his pleasure. Look at what he's done to you. It's not normal for a woman like you to be in a relationship with a sadist. You should end your relationship with him this instant." But Emily didn't want to end her relationship with Mr. Redd. She was under contract and couldn't return on a deal with him.

"Your mother and I are serious," said Mr. Richards.

"Well, I'm serious too," Emily said back. "Mr. Redd may be rough, but at least he's wealthy."

Her parents gave Emily a look of disappointment. "Money can't buy you happiness," Mrs. Richards said. "You need to be grateful for the life you once had." Emily didn't want to go back to her boring old life. She was happy with the luxury she had received in the past weeks. But it only made her parents upset.

"Before you met this, Mr. Redd, you were pure and innocent," said Mr. Richards. "We want you to end your relationship with him before he hurts you!"

Just then, Marcus came downstairs, overhearing the conversation. "You think this guy is your prince charming?" he said. "Man, you are a weirdo."

It made Emily angry. "Don't call me names," she yelled.

Mr. Richards told her to be quiet. "Don't insult your brother, Emily," he said.

"But he started it," Emily said.

"**LIAR**!" shouted Marcus.

"That's enough," Mr. Richards yelled. He sent Marcus out to buy milk while he continued his talk with Emily.

"Your luxurious lifestyle is taking you away from your family," he said. "This Mr. Redd is not to be trusted. Reflect on your life and your family."

Emily was upset with what her parents were saying. "I don't need you," she said. "You just don't trust me!"

Mr. Richards got up from his chair and approached Emily in a state of anger. "Emily Abigail Richards, you listen to me," he shouted. "One day, you will end up alone and have no one to blame but yourself."

Emily was tired of listening to her parents. "I hate you," she said. She left the living room and went to her room in a state of anger.

While she sat on her bed, she felt a little guilty about what she had said to her parents about Mr. Redd. She wondered if they were right and needed to end her relationship with him before something terrible happened. Emily picked up the telephone to call Mr. Redd. Luckily, she heard his voice on the other end of the line.

"Hello," said Emily.

Mr. Redd began to speak on the phone. "I was just finishing my workout," he said. "I'm so glad you called me," he added.

Emily interrupted him and wanted to share something important with him. "Mr. Redd, listen," she said.

However, Mr. Redd interrupted her and continued to discuss their next date. He told her he was taking her to a special place in Diablo City that night, inviting her to join him for dinner and dancing.

"Where are we having dinner?" asked Emily.

Emily and The Devil

"It's a surprise," said Mr. Redd on the phone. "I'll see you tonight at 7:00 pm. I'll pick you up in my limo." Emily hung up the phone and dressed for another date with Mr. Redd.

Later that evening, Emily came downstairs, wearing a royal blue midi dress with silver pumps. Emily looked at herself in the mirror and smiled. "I look very sexy," she thought. She began posing in front of the mirror like a model on the runway. But then, Marcus caught her from behind.

"What are you doing?" he said.

Emily was startled. "Marcus," she said.

Marcus looked at her in her blue dress and frowned. "You're not going out again, are you?" he asked.

Emily turned away from him in disgust. "That's none of your business," she said.

Marcus grabbed Emily by her arm and pinned her to the wall. "You're going to be in so much trouble," he said. "When I tell Mom and Dad that you're going out again, they're going to ground you."

Emily pushed her brother away. "I'm not a child, Marcus," she said.

"Yet you act like one," said Marcus in response.

Just then, the doorbell rang. "I'll get it," said Emily. She headed to the door and opened it. Mr. Redd stood in the doorway, wearing a black business shirt and dress pants.

He looked at Emily in her royal blue mini-dress and gave her a seductive glance. "Well, hello there," he said in a low, sexy voice.

Emily blushed. "Good evening, Sir," she said.

Mr. Redd kissed her on the lips because he was happy to see her after one week. "It's so good to see you again," he said. "And the blue dress looks gorgeous on you, my dear."

Emily giggled at Mr. Redd's compliment. "You're such a gentleman," she said.

Suddenly, Marcus interfered between the two. "You're not taking my sister away," he said. "I'm reporting you to the police!" Mr. Redd gave Marcus a cold, mean look.

"She's no longer your concern," he said. "Now go back to your room and watch TV."

Marcus got angry and punched Emily in the arm. "Mom and Dad are going to be mad with you when you come home tonight," he said.

"Are you in trouble now?"

Marcus went upstairs to his room and slammed the door. Emily was amazed at how Mr. Redd stood up to her brother like that. "You're so dominant," she said.

Mr. Redd smiled. "I do what I can to make sure no one takes you away from me," he said. "Now, about that dinner I promised you." Then, he took Emily by her hand and walked her to his car. He opened the door cordially. "After you," he said. Emily stepped into his vehicle, and Mr. Redd closed the door. Then, he got in and drove off.

Emily's parents stood and watched as their beloved daughter disappeared down the road in Mr. Redd's car. They returned to Diablo City as the sun was setting over the horizon. "Where are we going?" Emily asked.

"You'll see," Mr. Redd said. "We're going out for dinner and dancing tonight."

Emily was curious. "Dinner and dancing?" she asked.

Mr. Redd smiled. "Yes," he said. "I'm taking you to someplace special tonight."

Mr. Redd's car sped past the city's shimmering lights. As they headed to the Downtown area of Diablo City, Emily looked out the window to see the wonders of the city's nightlife. They soon arrived at a red-light district called "the Devil's Playground." A district where the streets form the shape of a devil's pitchfork.

"What is this place?" Emily said.

"This is the Devil's Playground," Mr. Redd said. "You remember the place I told you about the other night?"

Emily recalled him telling her about the Devil's Playground. She was about to experience it for the first time.

"Brace yourself, my dear," he said. Mr. Redd drove into the red-light district of Pitchfork Road, entering the Devil's Playground. Emily was amazed by the red-colored street. There were strip clubs, adult theaters, and nightclubs with a devilish theme. There were adult stores full of items made for couples. The mood was so tempting and enticing that it left Emily speechless. "Oh wow," Emily said with wonder. She had never seen a red light district before.

"See what you've been missing?" said Mr. Redd. "Everything your parents warned you to avoid is right there before your eyes." Then, Mr. Redd pointed towards a building on the left-hand side of the road.

"What is that?" Emily asked.

"This is my club," Mr. Redd said.

They arrived at a nightclub called The Redd House, which was established and owned by Mr. Redd. The exterior of the building was a 2-story structure with red lights and a red carpet near the entrance. Mr. Redd stopped the car and stepped out. He went around to the passenger side and opened the door. He took Emily by the hand and called a valet to park his car. Emily and Mr. Redd approached the club's front door, where a bouncer greeted them.

"Good evening, Sir," the bouncer said. "Who's your friend?"

Mr. Redd introduced Emily to him. "This is Emily Richards," he said. "She's my assistant." The bouncer smiled and welcomed Emily.

"Welcome to the Redd House," he said. He opened the door, and the two headed inside. Mr. Redd showed Emily the inside of the nightclub. The Redd House was thriving, with dancers and patrons enjoying themselves. It featured a large dance floor with elevated platforms, a bar, a DJ booth, and a seating area. Emily was enthralled and amazed by the lively atmosphere.

"It's incredible," she said. Mr.

Redd took her by the hand. "I own this club here in this part of town," he said. "It's voted number one in the top ten nightclubs weekly."

All the partygoers greeted Mr. Redd and told him about their great time at the club. Mr. Redd accepted their compliments and adoration. Emily looked at all the people, drawing Mr. Redd's attention. As they made their way through the crowd, they found a reserved table to sit at. When they sat down, Mr. Redd ordered drinks for himself and Emily. A bartender approached them.

"What can I get you, Sir?" he asked.

Mr. Redd pulled out a handful of dollars. "Two Inferno Cocktails," he responded. The bartender smiled and walked off. Mr. Redd looks at Emily. "Beautiful, isn't it?" he asked. Emily was breathless by the ambiance of the nightclub.

"My parents would flip their heads if they saw this place," she said.

Mr. Redd brought her face towards him. "Forget about your parents," he said. "You've got me now. Relax and enjoy. The night is young, and so are we."

Emily smiled. "You're right," she said. "They're not even here. They're probably back home sitting in the living room watching TV with my older brother." Both she and Mr. Redd laughed. Then, the bartender returned and brought them drinks. He received a tip from Mr. Redd in dollars.

"Thank you, Sir," said the bartender.

As he left, Mr. Redd offered Emily a drink. "A toast to the night," he said. They took a sip from their drinks in celebration. A few minutes later, a host appeared on stage and introduced the next act.

"Good evening, Ladies and Gentlemen," he said on the microphone. "Welcome to the Redd House. Please welcome to the stage: The Kittens." Applause from the crowd filled the room as a band appeared on stage. They began to play a song. While the music was playing, Mr. Redd ordered dinner for the two of them. A waitress came to their table and placed two plates before them. As Emily was having dinner, Mr. Redd offered a glass of wine.

"How are you enjoying the dinner?" he asked. Emily swallowed before she could answer.

"It's good," she said. Emily took a sip of wine from the glass before finishing her dinner. As the band finished playing, they left the stage with the sound of applause. Then, Mr. Redd took the stage and introduced himself to the audience.

"Hello, everyone," he said. "I want to sing a song for you. This song is for my dear lady, who is here tonight. Miss Emily Richards." Mr. Redd signaled the band members to start playing. "Hit it, boys," he said. Everyone cheered as Mr. Redd began to sing a song for the people.

The band behind him provided the music. Emily was surprised to hear Mr. Redd sing. Her jaw dropped in amazement. "Is there anything he can't do?" she thought. A woman sitting next to her leaned over and whispered in her ear. "I've seen him play piano," she said. "But I never thought I'd hear him sing." Emily was utterly speechless, watching Mr. Redd sing on stage. Mr. Redd saw Emily's reaction and smiled as he approached her while singing. His hips swayed with the music, allowing him to pour his sexiness towards the audience. Ladies swooned at the sound of his voice. Emily swooned more. She thought it was the wine that was making her feverish. Her face was flushed, and she was lightheaded. Her eyes focused on Mr. Redd's eyes while he was singing. He gave her a seductive wink and a smile and blew her a kiss. Emily blushed bright red from his seduction.

As soon as he finished, everyone applauded. Mr. Redd returned to his seat and looked at Emily. "Enjoy the show?" he asked.

Emily closed her mouth and blushed. "I..um...well, I...liked it," she said.

Mr. Redd touched her cheek with his hand. "Left you speechless, I see," he said.

Emily's eyes widened. "I've never heard you sing before," she said.

Mr. Redd laughed. "You will get used to it," he said. "Usually, I enjoy a little song and dance anywhere." Then, he kissed her on the lips. It made Emily feel warm all over. Soon, the music changed, and everyone got onto the dance floor. "Care to dance with me?" Mr. Redd asked.

"Sure," replied Emily. Mr. Redd took Emily by the hand, and they danced for the rest of the night as the music played. The music was loud, and the people danced together on the dance floor.

Emily felt excited dancing with Mr. Redd in a nightclub. "I wish this night wouldn't end," she said.

Mr. Redd grinned. "Of course, my dear," he said. Everyone watched the two of them dance together, unaware that the mirror behind them reflected Mr. Redd's image. In the mirror, a red-skinned devil danced with Emily. They were shocked to see something like this in a nightclub. But a cloud of red mist fogged the mirror, and everyone became entranced. They resumed dancing amid red fog. Mr. Redd laughed as he looked over at the crowd behind him, a sinister look appearing on his face. Emily looked up at him and caught his attention.

"What's so funny?" she asked.

Mr. Redd pulled her towards him and kissed her on the lips. "Just enjoy the music," he said. His kiss left Emily drunk. But they continued dancing. His hands began to touch all over Emily's body sensually. Emily ground her hips into his very slowly. Mr. Redd moaned in her ear. She was turning him on. "You are a fucking tease," he said. His hands reached up to her breasts and began to squeeze them gently. Emily gasped at his touch. "Does that feel good?" Mr. Redd asked.

"Oh, please," Emily whispered. "I'm going to faint."

Mr. Redd wrapped his arm around her and pulled her to him. "Let your fantasies unwind," he said. The two embraced each other on the dance floor all night.

Later, Emily and Mr. Redd left the Redd House and returned to the car. Everyone said "goodnight" to him as they were going. "Come back anytime," said the bouncer. They got into his car and drove off down the road. They returned to Mr. Redd's penthouse for the remainder of the evening. Emily was so exhausted from the dance that she collapsed onto the couch. She was still feeling lightheaded from dancing all night and barely managed to stand up. Mr. Redd offered Emily a glass of wine, and she drank it. Soon, she began to hiccup from the wine. Mr. Redd laughed and took Emily to his playroom. He goes over to the closet and pulls out another sexy outfit for Emily to wear—a sheer red nightgown with black fishnet stockings and a red satin thong. "Put it on," he said. Emily looks at the outfit carefully. "Why do you want me to wear this?" she asked.

"So I can watch you dance," Mr. Redd replied. Emily wasn't sure. She was too tired to dance. Mr. Redd growled at Emily for refusing to put on the outfit. "Put it on," he said.

Emily had no choice but to agree to wear the outfit for Mr. Redd. First, she puts on the stockings. Next, she puts on the thong. And finally, she puts on the nightgown. Mr. Redd noticed her outfit and smiled. "You look beautiful," he said. He sits down on the leather couch. Then, he gives her some instructions to follow. "Dance for me," he said. He points to a circular stage with a pole in the center. Emily looked at the stage and raised an eyebrow. "You want me to dance on that?" she asked. "Yes," said Mr. Redd. "I want you to dance for me on that stage." Emily walks over to the stage and steps up to it. Then, she begins to dance for him. She was a little shy to be dancing for a grown man in a playroom.

Mr. Redd grinned as he watched Emily dance for him. Unzipping his pants with one hand, he began to masturbate. He imagined feeling Emily's body pressed against his as he stroked his big, long cock quietly while Emily danced on the small, circular stage. Then, he tells her to strip out of her night gown and her thong, but keep her stockings on. She did as she obeyed. Emily slid the straps off her shoulder and let the night gown slide down her body, exposing her naked flesh as Mr. Redd continued to stroke his cock faster. Next, Emily removed her thong and tossed it aside. Mr. Redd moaned louder and louder until he released a heavy load. Suddenly, Emily stopped dancing and stood before him completely naked. Mr.

Redd got up from the chair and took her off the stage. Mr. Redd watched her hungrily, studying her body. He found it erotically intoxicating. "Delicious," he said. "You look delicious."

Emily flushed as Mr. Redd looked at her body. Then, Mr. Redd instructs her to lie down on the bondage bed. "Go lie down on the bed," he said. Emily obeyed and walked to the bondage bed. She lies down on her back as Mr. Redd begins to bind her ankles and wrists to the posts with leather cuffs. Then, he removes his shirt, pants, and underwear to be naked with her. He straddles Emily and kisses her with passion, not aggression. Then, he begins to have sex with her. He tightened the cuffs on Emily's wrists and ankles. "Not too hard," she cried. "It's the effects of your little show," he said. "I said you were a fucking tease, and I meant it." Then, he leans down to bite her on the neck. Emily let out a cry as Mr. Redd penetrated her on the bed. The sound of his skin slapping against hers in rhythmic motions. His hot lips moved down her collarbone and onto her chest. Emily moaned louder as her body writhed in pain and pleasure. Mr. Redd pounded faster and harder. The bed shook as he was close to orgasm. His mouth on Emily's breast sent shivers down her spine. His hand grabbed the other breast and squeezed tightly. The sensation was bringing Emily to the edge of orgasm.

When they finished, Mr. Redd kissed her and wiped away her tears. Emily went to sleep with her mind as blank as a painter's canvas, as Mr. Redd uncuffed her from the bed and carried her into his bedroom so she could rest. As Emily slept, he sat down on the chair and began to masturbate again. He didn't want to wake her. Then, he got up from his chair and sat down on the bed next to her. He kissed her on the lips as he continued to stroke his cock faster until he released his heaviest load of cum onto the sheets. When he finished, he went to sleep with Emily in his bed.

The next morning, Emily woke up from a dream she had. She got out of bed and put on one of Mr. Redd's robes from the closet. She left his bedroom and went into the living room, where she found Mr. Redd dancing to some music playing on the stereo. Emily stood and watched. But then, Mr. Redd saw Emily standing there and smiled.

"Emily," he said. "What a surprise."

Emily laughed. "I see you're dancing up a storm," she said. Mr. Redd offered her a dance. The two began to dance in the living room together. But then, Emily noticed the time on the clock. It was already 8:45 am. "Oh no," she said. "I'm late!" She stopped dancing with him and rushed to get dressed; however, Mr. Redd stopped her from doing so.

"Don't hurry, baby," he said. "We have all the time in the world." He kissed her on the lips and wrapped his arms around her.

Emily stopped him from kissing her so she could speak. "You don't understand," she said. "If I'm not home, I'll be in big trouble." Mr. Redd silenced her without another kiss.

"Forget about your home," he said. "You belong to me." Emily pulls away and goes into the bedroom to get dressed. A few minutes later, Emily left the room fully dressed and went to the door. Mr. Redd looked at her, confused. "What's the matter?" he asked. "Don't you want to dance with me?"

Emily shook her head in response. "Please, take me home," she said. Mr. Redd sighed and walked her to the elevator. They went inside as the elevator doors closed. They left the penthouse and went into Mr. Redd's limo. He drove Emily home to Halo Town. Then, they arrived in front of Emily's house, and Emily stepped out of Mr. Redd's limo. She said "goodbye" to him and closed the door. Mr. Redd watched from the window.

"I'll see you again," he said. The limo drove away.

When Emily came home, she was in a state of shock. Her parents called Emily into the living room. "Yes," said Emily. "You wanted to see me?"

Emily's parents were angry at her. They found a picture of her on their front porch this morning. "What is the meaning of this?" Mr. Richards asked. Emily saw the picture and got scared. It was a picture of herself and Mr. Redd dancing at the Redd House from last night. She saw how she was dancing next to him in a sexual manner.

"Please, Dad," she said. "I can explain."

Mr. Richards slammed the picture on the table in anger. "Don't, 'I can explain' me, young lady," he replied. "Why were you at a nightclub?"

Emily tried to answer his question. However, Marcus then entered the room. He was just as angry as her parents were. "I bet it has something to do with Mr. Redd," he said. "She probably slept with him and had sex with him."

Both her parents gasped. Their gaze turned to Emily with anger. "You had sex with him?" Mr. Richards asked.

"I didn't know," said Emily. "He forced me to do it with him. I couldn't just say 'no' to him."

Mr. Richards became furious. His eyes burned bright red at his daughter. "**THAT'S ENOUGH**!!" he yelled.

"Emily Richards, you are in big trouble! We warned you about this man," Mrs. Richards said. "We are incredibly disappointed in you! You disobeyed us when we specifically told you not to go out with this man."

Marcus grinned at Emily and started to tease her. "You are so busted," he said.

Emily was shocked. "You told them," she said.

"I did not," said Marcus. "You brought this on yourself."

Emily got angry at him. She picked up a pillow and threw it at him. Mr. Richards stopped Emily and smacked her in the face. "This has gone too far," he said. "You will go to your room and think about what you've done. You must never go out with this man again!"

Emily couldn't accept the pressure of hatred from her parents and older brother. "I wish you would all just go away," she yelled. So she went upstairs to her room and closed the door. Emily collapsed onto the bed and started to cry.

That afternoon, Emily was still in her room, crying. She was still upset with her parents after her fight with them when she came home. She looked out the window and watched the sunset over the horizon. Emily sat down on the bed and sighed. Just then, the telephone rang. Emily answered it to see who was calling.

"Hello," she said.

"Emily," said Mr. Redd, calling from his office. "How are you feeling?"

Emily wiped away her tears before she could speak. "My parents are mad at me because of the picture they saw," she said. "They said I shouldn't go out with you anymore."

Mr. Redd laughed. "That's ridiculous," he said. "Of course, your parents want you to go out with me. Isn't that why you signed the contract?"

Emily thought about it at first. She remembered the contract she had signed and knew that she couldn't go back on it. "Don't cry," said Mr. Redd. "How about I take you on another date to get your mind off your parents tonight?"

Emily said she would love the idea.

Later that evening, Mr. Redd arrived at Emily's house in his car. Emily left her home and got into his car. They drove off and returned to Mr. Redd's penthouse in Diablo City. As they headed inside, Mr. Redd and Emily shared a passionate kiss in the living room. Mr. Redd sat Emily down on the couch and removed her shoes. "Have I got something for you?" Mr. Redd said. He brings Emily to his playroom for another night of BDSM sex. He locked the door behind him and walked over to the closet. He pulled out his red key and opened the door. A few minutes later, he came out with a handful of bondage rope. Emily looked at the rope nervously.

"What's it for?" she asked. Mr. Redd approached her as he unfurled the rope in his hands.

"You," he said. He tightened the rope around Emily's neck like a collar. "On your knees," he demanded.

Emily got on her knees as Mr. Redd stepped back, letting out the rope like a leash. "Come to me," he said. Emily crawled up to him until her face met his lower waist. Mr. Redd stripped Emily naked and brought her to the whipping bench. Next, he secured her ankles and wrists with the red rope as he prepared her for his pleasure. He pulled out a flogger and ran the material along her back. "Feel that?" he asked. Emily gasped slightly as she noticed her reflection in the mirror. When she saw Mr. Redd's reflection, he looked different. His skin was red, and he had horns. But as she was about to turn around to get a look at him, Mr. Redd began to flog her on the butt. **"WHIP!"**

"Ouch!" cried Emily. The stinging pain of the flogger was so sharp that it made Emily flinch. Mr. Redd flogged her again. "WHIP!" The flogger was extremely sharp, like barbed wire to flesh. Mr. Redd repeatedly flogged her multiple times. "WHIP! WHIP!" Emily's butt was left wholly bruised and scarred.

After he finished, Mr. Redd put the flogger down and approached Emily. He stood before the mirror to prevent her from seeing his reflection. He made Emily give him a blowjob on his cock to get him erect and hard before he could have sex with her.

Mr. Redd moaned and groaned as Emily's mouth surrounded his massive cock. He couldn't wait much longer. He pulled his cock out of her mouth. Then, he went behind Emily and began to penetrate her in her butt while he let his hand play with her clitoris. Emily whimpered and moaned from the pleasure and pain to the point where she couldn't control herself. Mr. Redd pulled on the red rope leash tight, like he was pulling the reins of a horse.

"Don't come yet," he said. He continued playing with Emily's clitoris, leaving her to whimper and moan in ecstasy. The two orgasmed, and Emily was left breathless. Mr. Redd loosened the rope and removed Emily from the whipping bench. Then, he brought her over to the bondage bed. He lay her down and secured her wrists and ankles with leather cuffs. Mr. Redd straddled her and began to penetrate her on top. "Do you still want your life of luxury?" he asked. "Yes, I do," Emily replied. Mr. Redd gripped her tighter before he gave his warning. "If you want to keep your life of luxury, you will let me fuck you," he said. "After we've fucked, you can never see your family again. Otherwise, I could never allow you to live another day with me."

Emily gasped for air, hearing Mr. Redd telling her never to see her family again. "Unless I never see my family again?" she asked. Mr. Redd leans in towards her. His eyes met hers with fire. "Yes," he said. "If I picture them in our lives, I could never achieve satisfaction for you." Emily wasn't sure whether to agree with Mr. Redd's demands. "My parents would be upset if I never saw them again," she said. Mr. Redd grabs her neck again. "Don't you love me?" he asked. "Of course," replied Emily. "Don't you want me?" Mr. Redd asked. "Yes," Emily answered. Mr. Redd's hand gripped Emily's neck tighter as he began to penetrate her.

"Then, say you will never see your family again," he said. "Never?" said Emily. "Never," Mr. Redd growled. Then, he leans down to bite her on the neck. The thrusting movements of his hips hit Emily in all the right spots. Suddenly, Emily's thoughts of her parents start to echo in her mind. She looked at their images in the mirror. They looked disappointed to see what Emily was doing. The image vanished, and Emily's eyes filled with tears.

Emily and The Devil

Mr. Redd grabs her face and forces her to look at him in his eyes. "Never see your family again," he growled. Emily tried to look away, but she couldn't stop looking into Mr. Redd's eyes. He was serious about making her forget about her family. He penetrated her harder to make her forget. Emily shut her eyes tightly, and the memories of her family disappeared from her mind as she reached orgasm. They orgasmed again and again until they were exhausted. Mr. Redd uncuffed Emily's wrists and ankles and removed her from the bondage bed. They left the playroom and went into Mr. Redd's bedroom. Emily lay down on Mr. Redd's bed and fell asleep. Her body was still shaking from the multiple orgasms she received.

# Chapter 9

The next day, Mr. Redd took Emily to Halo University in his limo. While on the road, he gave her a red bag with pink tissue paper. "What is this?" she asked.

Mr. Redd looked at her with a smile. "Open it," he said. Emily opened the bag and found an outfit. It was a wine-red mini dress with matching pumps and black fishnet stockings.

Emily looked at Mr. Redd, confused. "Why are you giving me this?" she asked him.

"I want you to wear it at college," Mr. Redd replied. "And I want to see you at my office when my limo comes to pick you up this afternoon."

Emily wasn't sure about this. "I can't wear it to college," she said.

"Yes, you are," said Mr. Redd. "You will wear this sexy outfit for me and I want you to look sexy in it." Emily felt threatened to hear Mr. Redd demanding her. Suddenly, he told his driver to stop the limo and pull over to a nearby alleyway.

The limo driver responded and drove up to an empty alleyway where no one could see them. Mr. Redd straddled Emily and undressed her in the backseat of his limo.

"What are you doing?" Emily cried as she struggled to escape. Mr. Redd grabbed her wrists before she reached the door handle.

"I'm gonna fuck you, you naughty bitch," he said.

Then, he kissed her hard and aggressively to make Emily submit. As he continued to remove her clothes, he began to penetrate her like a sexually aggressive animal.

"You want to keep your life of luxury?" he asked. Emily's muffled words reached his ears as his hands grabbed her breasts. She could feel his hot breath on her skin as he penetrated her hard and fast in the backseat of his limo. Moaning and groaning, Mr. Redd pounded harder into Emily as she let out wave after wave of orgasms.

When they finished, Mr. Redd adjusted his clothes, and Emily put on the provocative outfit he had given her. She felt embarrassed to be wearing something like this. Mr. Redd growled with pleasure at the sight of her. "You look sexy," he said. He leaned over to her ear and licked her. "I can't wait to see you in my office wearing that outfit," he whispered. He informed the driver to take them to Halo Town.

A few minutes later, the limo arrived at Halo University. Emily stepped out of the limo wearing the outfit Mr. Redd had given her. She looked more like a stripper than a student on campus. Her face turned red with embarrassment. "I don't know if I should be doing this," she said.

Mr. Redd smacked her on her butt. "Don't keep me waiting," he said sternly. Soon, he closed the door and drove off down the road.

Emily approached the campus clutching her backpack. Suddenly, everyone stopped to look at her. They saw Emily wearing provocative clothes and questioned her.

"Emily, what are you wearing?" one of the students asked. Emily looked at them nervously.

"It's how Mr. Redd wants me to dress for him now," she said. The college students were amazed to hear that Mr. Redd had made Emily wear provocative clothes on campus.

Suddenly, Nicole, Jetta, and Katie approached Emily, angry. They saw Emily's provocative clothes and thought she was getting all the attention from the college students.

"**EMILY**!!!" Nicole shouted. "How dare you come to college wearing that attire and getting every guy for yourself?"

Emily looked at Nicole and frowned. "What's the matter? Jealous?" she said. Nicole gasped at Emily's response.

"Don't think I don't know what you're doing," she said. "Because I am going to tell Professor Phillips about you, and she is going to have your ass expelled!"

Emily frowned at Nicole. She didn't like how mean she was to her. "You're just a jealous bitch," she said.

Nicole grew furious. "Your relationship with Mr. Redd has turned you into a whore," said Nicole. "I bet you had sex with him, which is why you're wearing those slutty clothes!"

Just then, Professor Phillips appeared. "What is going on here?" she said. Nicole told the student body about Emily's relationship with Mr. Redd on campus.

"Emily had sex with Mr. Redd," she said. "And he's making her wear these atrocious clothes."

Professor Phillips looked at Emily and gasped. "Emily Richards," she said. "Is this true? Are you in a relationship with a man?"

Emily looked at Professor Phillips in fear. "Yes, I am," she answered. All the students gasped. Professor Phillips was shocked to hear about Emily's relationship with Mr. Redd.

"Ms. Emily Richards," she said. "I will not tolerate such provocative behavior on campus. You're coming with me." She brought Emily inside the building and took her to the Dean's office. Professor Phillips explained to Dean Woodrow about her provocative outfit and her relationship with Mr. Redd. Dean Woodrow was angry. He told Emily never to wear inappropriate clothes to college again, or else she would be expelled from Halo University. As Emily left the Dean's office, she sadly headed to the bathroom to change into her regular casual clothes. She came out of the ladies' restroom in the plain, regular clothes she had brought from home and made her way to class for the remainder of the day.

Later that evening, Emily came home and saw her parents in the living room. They were furious with her. Mr. Richards approached and told Emily to go into the living room.

"The Dean called today," he said. "He told us you wore a provocative outfit to college."

Emily's eyes filled with tears as she heard her father's voice, bitter and harsh. Then, without warning, Mr. Richards smacked Emily in the face with brute force. "What were you thinking?" he yelled.

"I didn't know," Emily cried. "Mr. Redd made me wear that outfit. It was his decision. Not mine."

Mrs. Richards stood next to Mr. Richards, facing Emily. "You know you're not allowed to wear anything indecent to college," she said. "I thought we agreed that you would end your relationship with Mr. Redd. Did you forget?" Emily tried to tell them about her relationship and how long she had been with Mr. Redd, having been together for only a few days. However, it led them to greater hatred.

Mr. Richards grabbed Emily's bag and pulled out the sexy outfit Mr. Redd had given her. "This outfit is not to be worn in public," he yelled. He threw it into the fire and grabbed Emily's arm. "You can't wear anything provocative or go to any strip clubs. You are 19 years old and still a minor!" He dragged her out of the couch. "Go to your room, Emily," he said. "We cannot allow you to go on any more dates with this man ever again. Do you understand? *NEVER AGAIN*!!"

Emily sadly went upstairs to her room. As she did, she sat down on the bed and began to cry. Just then, the phone rang. Mr. Redd was calling. But Emily didn't want to answer it. Her parents told her to never go on another date with him. She ignored his call and went to sleep.

The next day, Emily awoke and got dressed in her casual college clothes. A pink sweater and a pair of blue jeans. She felt upset about what had happened at Halo University the previous day. She remembered what her parents had told her about Mr. Redd and why she should never go out with him. She also recalled being told never to wear sexy lingerie or provocative outfits to college by the Dean and Professor Phillips. Before she left her room, she saw that her phone had 12 messages from Mr. Redd. Emily played one of them to hear what they had to say.

"Emily," said Mr. Redd's voice message. "I'm inviting you to a Board meeting at my office. I want you there in 5 minutes." Emily played another message. Each message played showed Mr. Redd's impatience in his voice. So Emily erased them.

Just then, the door opened. Her mother was standing in the doorway. "Emily, you're going to be late," she said. Emily faced her, looking scared. She sighed as she left her room. Mrs. Richards didn't hug her. Instead, she hit her on the back of her head in anger. "Don't wear any more indecent sexual outfits again," she said.

"Yes, Mom," replied Emily sadly. Afterwards, she left the house and closed the door.

At Halo University, Emily kept feeling the pain her parents inflicted on her. The students on campus gave her mean looks after what happened yesterday when she arrived in Mr. Redd's limousine. In computer class, Emily was taking a test on the computer. Suddenly, she sees an email sent from Redd Enterprises, Inc. She opened the email and found a message from Mr. Redd. The message read: "Emily, why didn't you show up at my office last night? I've been waiting for hours for you to show up in that sexy outfit I gave you. Also, why haven't you called me back? Are you ignoring your duties as my submissive? If you are, I will come over to your house and bring you to my office." Emily didn't reply to the message. She quickly deleted it and went back to taking the test.

Later that afternoon, Emily came home. Her body was shaking with fear at the thought of what her parents might say. As she opened the door, she found the house empty. Emily sighed with relief. "They're not home," she thought. She sat down on the couch to do her homework. But then, there was a knock on the door. "Who could that be?" she thought. She got up to answer it. To her surprise, she saw Mr. Redd in the doorway, wearing his red office suit. He looked angry at Emily. He was not pleased.

Emily's face flushed at the sight of him. "What are you doing here?" she asked. Mr. Redd forced his way into Emily's house as he approached her angrily.

"Why didn't you show up at my office yesterday?" he asked. "I've been waiting for you for 8 hours!"

Emily shook her head in fear. "I didn't want to come to your office," she said. However, Mr. Redd continued to approach Emily angrily.

"We had a deal," he said. "You were supposed to come to my office! You didn't call me back after I called you 12 times!!"

Emily told him she wasn't allowed to go on any more dates with him because her parents were upset with her. However, Mr. Redd then noticed that Emily wasn't wearing the provocative outfit. "Where is it?" he asked.

Emily swallowed. "Where's what?" she said.

Mr. Redd's eyes fixed on Emily in a heated glare of anger. "Where's the outfit I gave you?" he said. "I specifically said for you to wear the sexy outfit I gave you! Where is it?"

Emily shut her eyes to hide her tears. Then, she spoke. "My parents threw it out," she said.

Mr. Redd got surprised. "What?" he said.

"They told me I can't wear anything inappropriate to college ever again," Emily said. But Mr. Redd didn't care about what her parents told her. He was more upset with how she ignored his demands.

"I gave you that outfit to wear all day," he said. "Not to have it tossed in the trash by your parents!!" Emily tried to explain, but to no avail. Mr. Redd picked her up and brought her over his shoulder. Then, he brought her to his car outside and threw her into the back seat. Slamming the door, he got into the driver's seat and drove off down the road. They arrived in Diablo City, and Mr. Redd drove her to the Luxuria Apartment. He took her upstairs to his penthouse to teach her a lesson about tardiness and ignorance. He brought Emily to his playroom and sat down on a red leather couch. Then, he put Emily on his lap and pulled down her pants, showing her butt. He took out a paddle and spanked her butt hard.

"This is for keeping me waiting," he said. "This is for ignoring my phone calls. And this is for having your sexy outfit thrown away!" When he finished, he picked up Emily and sat her down on the couch. "Next time, don't keep me waiting," he growled. Emily's eyes filled with tears. Mr. Redd grabbed her neck and squeezed her throat. "Do I make myself clear?" he said.

"Yes, Sir," Emily replied.

"Good girl," said Mr. Redd. Then, he let go and put down the paddle. Suddenly, the telephone rang. Mr. Redd went to answer it. "Don't move," he said. He opened the door to answer the phone.

"Hello," he said.

Emily and The Devil

Emily's father, Mr. Richards, called Mr. Redd on the phone. He was asking about Emily. "Where is my daughter?" he asked. "I want to speak to her!"

Mr. Redd grinned wickedly. "Emily can't come to the phone tonight," he said. "She belongs to me. She's mine." Then, he hung up the phone and returned to the playroom. He still wanted to make Emily forget about her family.

As the days passed, Emily and Mr. Redd continued their relationship together. Mr. Redd took Emily to Halo University in his limo every day. Every night, Emily would go out with him to nightclubs and come to his penthouse instead of coming home to her family. As the days passed, Emily grew increasingly concerned with Mr. Redd's demands. However, their relationship was creating conflict among students, professors, and her family both on and off campus. Her relationship with Mr. Redd had become a problem because he was encouraging her to do things that no ordinary person would do. He made her do things for his pleasure, which included buying and wearing lingerie under her clothes as daily wear, joining him for nights in his playroom to explore more of his world of BDSM, and satisfying his sexual needs. He also had Emily arrange meetings with people to bring to his office for potential deals. Mr. Redd rewarded Emily for her duties by having sex with her in his playroom afterwards. Emily fell deeper and deeper into Mr. Redd's clutches without realizing it.

Later that evening, Emily went on another date with Mr. Redd. They went back to the Redd House for another party. Mr. Redd ordered drinks for both Emily and himself. Emily didn't feel like having a drink. She felt depressed about her relationship. Emily was getting tired of being Mr. Redd's submissive. She wanted their relationship to end. She didn't want to get into any more trouble at home or at Halo University.

One month later, in September, in Mr. Redd's penthouse, Emily woke up in Mr. Redd's bed completely naked. She tried to get up, but her body ached from the pain. Suddenly, Mr. Redd entered the bedroom. "Good morning," he said. "Sleep well?"

Emily looked at him. "No, I didn't," she said.

Mr. Redd came up to her. "Poor Princess," he said. "I know what will make you feel better. A nice, soothing bath."

Emily stopped him for a minute so she could speak. "I think we should stop seeing each other," she said. But Mr. Redd stopped her before she could explain why they shouldn't be together.

"I want you to bathe with me," he said. "My tub is waiting for us." Emily was frustrated. How could she explain to Mr. Redd that she no longer wanted to see him? Emily needed to make her explanation gentle and straightforward, without upsetting Mr. Redd.

So Emily got out of bed and joined Mr. Redd in the bathroom. Mr. Redd had filled the tub with warm water and bubbles. Mr. Redd bathed Emily, providing her with special treatment. He gently cleansed her skin with fragrant soap and a soft, yielding sponge, ensuring that every inch of her body was revitalized and refreshed. But as he did, he began to touch her body sensually. Emily moaned from his touch in the bathtub. The soap and water, mixed with a sweet fragrance, left her feeling dazed. Mr. Redd leaned over and kissed her. His breath tickled her flesh as his hands caressed her body in the water. Mr. Redd straddled Emily and penetrated her in the bathtub. The splashing sound of water from the tub mingled with their writhing in pleasure. Then, they got out of the tub and dried themselves with clean, fluffy towels. Mr. Redd gave her some clothes to wear. She wore a satin royal blue dress suit with white matte pumps and matching gloves. At the same time, Mr. Redd wore the same red suit he had worn when he met Emily.

After Emily wore her new, clean clothes, Mr. Redd took her to the living room, where they would watch a movie together. Mr. Redd turned on the TV and sat on the couch next to Emily as they watched the movie. But then, Mr. Redd looked at Emily. "What's the matter?" he asked.

Emily started to cry a little as she turned to him and answered his question. "I think we should stop seeing each other," she said.

Mr. Redd asked her why.

Emily looked up at him at first, but then she lowered her head in sadness. "My parents were upset with me because of our relationship," she said. "They said you're dangerous, and our relationship makes things difficult for me." Mr. Redd didn't believe her.

"That's ridiculous," he said. "What makes you think I'm a danger?"

Emily showed him the scars on her body that he gave her a couple of nights ago. "They asked me questions about you, and I didn't tell them," she said. "They're concerned about me. They want me to end our sexual relationship. I don't want to be your sex slave."

Mr. Redd was confused. "Who said I was making you my sex slave?" he asked. Emily mentioned the day he made her wear a provocative outfit to college, which got her in trouble with her parents. But Mr. Redd didn't care how much trouble she was in. He cared more about having Emily stay with him in his penthouse as his submissive.

"I specifically said that you can never see your family again," he said. "Have you forgotten?"

But Emily looked at Mr. Redd with an angry look on her face. "You're a sadist, Mr. Redd," she said. "I thought you were a gentleman. But I was wrong. I don't want to see you again."

Mr. Redd was disappointed. "Are you breaking up with me?" he asked.

Emily nodded. "Yes, I am breaking up with you," she replied. "I don't want to be your sex slave anymore. I'm not a prisoner. I'm a human being, and I deserve to be treated with respect and dignity. Okay?"

Mr. Redd felt heartbroken hearing Emily tell him she wanted to end their relationship. He didn't want her to leave. "After everything I've given you, you want to break up with me?" he asked.

Emily answered, "Yes." She wanted their relationship to end.

Mr. Redd grew angry at Emily for rejecting him. "You wanted to be like a princess," he said. "I gave you everything. I gave you new clothes, jewelry, and the finest necessities I bought for you, and this is the thanks I get?" His voice echoed throughout the room, making Emily shake with fear.

"Listen, Mr. Redd," said Emily. "This relationship has turned into a nightmare, and I don't want to continue."

Mr. Redd tried to change her mind by acting nice. "But don't you want to stay?" he asked.

Emily shook her head. "No," she answered. "I don't want to stay with you."

Mr. Redd frowned at Emily's suggestion of ending their relationship. He didn't want her to leave him. "May I remind you of our agreement?" he said.

Emily remembered the deal she had made, but was more worried about her parents. "I'm sorry, Mr. Redd," she told him. "But I think we should stop seeing each other. No more late-night meetings or any BDSM sex nights in the playroom." Emily got up from the couch and began to leave. But Mr. Redd stopped her from leaving before she reached the door.

"You can't leave me," he said. "What about our deal? You don't want to return to your boring, pitiful life, right?"

Emily didn't look at Mr. Redd. She didn't want him to see her cry. Mr. Redd brought his face close to hers and looked into her eyes, tears filling his own. "Don't look so sad," he said. "No need for tears." He kissed her. But she turned away.

"No," she said. Mr. Redd grabbed her arms firmly.

"I wasn't kidding when I said I liked you," he said. "I do, Emily." His grip was leaving blisters on her arm. It was hurting her so much that she started to cry again. "I want you to stay here with me," Mr. Redd said. "You are my submissive, after all."

But Emily broke away from his grip. "Mr. Redd," she said. "There's no room in my life for someone like you."

Mr. Redd didn't believe her. "You're lying," he said. Mr. Redd grabbed her breast and squeezed it firmly in his hand. "You love it when I touch you, Emily," he said in a deep, seductive voice. "If you stay with me, I can give you more of that sweet, sexual sensation."

However, Emily pushed Mr. Redd away the second time and headed for the door. "Goodbye, Mr. Redd," she said. "I must go home now before my parents wonder where I am." So Emily turned away and left the penthouse to go home.

Mr. Redd frowned. "You'll be back," he said. "No matter where you go, you will come back to me. I'll be waiting for you when you return." Emily didn't look back. She headed into the elevator without saying another word to him. Mr. Redd was left heartbroken as he watched Emily leave his penthouse. He wanted to get her back one way or another. Outside, Emily called a taxi to drive her home to Halo Town. She tried to tell her parents how sorry she was for disobeying them.

The next day, Emily was at Halo University, researching relationships on the computer. She wanted to ensure that her facts were correct. Emily was surprised when the Redd Enterprises website suddenly appeared on the screen. She opened the file. Then, she saw a video of Mr. Redd whipping Emily in the playroom a few nights ago. Emily was shocked. She couldn't believe what she was seeing. "Oh no," Emily said. She attempted to switch it off but was unsuccessful. The video quickly went viral. Everyone on campus was watching it on their computers. Even Dean Woodrow and Professor Phillips saw the video on their laptops in their offices.

Emily panicked as all the students turned to look at her. They were shocked to the core. Emily's heart raced as the students began to call her distasteful names. It made Emily feel uncomfortable under the students' stares and whispers. She left the classroom to escape from the voices of every student. But the whispers grew louder, and the words became more apparent. "Emily, the whore! Emily, the whore!" She wondered if this was Mr. Redd's doing. "Is he blackmailing me?" she thought. "Could he be doing this to get me back to him?"

Suddenly, Emily saw pictures of herself on the walls of the hallway. All of them read, "Emily the whore!" and feature Emily wearing the naughty schoolgirl outfit, posing in a provocative position. The pictures were by Mr. Redd, who received the picture Emily had sent him the other day. Everyone on campus saw them and turned their gaze to Emily. One student approached her with a stern look on his face. "Is this you?" he asked, pointing at the picture on the wall. Emily shook her head in denial.

"That's not me," she said. "Someone must have played a trick on them." But no one believed her. The person in the picture was Emily. Every student looked at her. They began to chant, "Emily the whore!" as they came closer to her in the form of a mob. Emily was scared. All the students surrounded her. She fled the building in fear. Emily ran down the street to her house. Along the way, she saw more pictures of her in every building. A video of her and Mr. Redd was on every store TV screen. She wanted to block out everyone's voices. However, they grew louder and louder.

That night, Emily was asleep. Suddenly, she woke up. Emily felt her heart racing as she sat in bed, tears welling in her eyes. Her whole body started to shake with fear. Just then, her phone rang. Emily answers it.

"Hello," she said in a broken voice.

Mr. Redd was calling from his penthouse. "Emily," he said. "Are you feeling okay?"

Emily told him she was not okay. "I had a terrible dream," she said. "Everyone on campus saw that video on their computers. They even saw my picture in that schoolgirl outfit you made me wear. Even my parents saw the picture and got mad at me."

Mr. Redd stopped her for a minute to speak to her. "You should come back to me," he said. "You know how much I miss you."

Emily gasped. "Did you upload a video of us having sex on the internet?" she asked him.

Mr. Redd denied her question. "I don't know what you're talking about," he said. Emily told him about the video she saw at college today.

"Everyone called me a whore because of that video and the pictures," she said. "Did you have anything to do with it?"

But Mr. Redd shrugged off the question. "You do need to come back to me," he said. "I can help you forget all the hatred everyone has given you. All you need to do is say "Yes.""

Emily gasped. "You *ARE* blackmailing me," she said. "I won't do it!" Mr. Redd didn't want to accept her refusal. He still wanted her to return to his penthouse.

"Don't play coy with me," he said. Emily wasn't kidding. She wanted an answer from Mr. Redd.

"I want to know if you had anything to do with the video you posted," she said.

But Mr. Redd still didn't answer her question. "Don't be cruel," he said. "Come to my penthouse, Emily, so that we can continue our relationship."

However, Emily refused to return to him. She promised never to see him again to avoid getting in trouble with her parents. "I'm not coming back to you," she said. "I said that we would never see each other again, and I meant it."

Mr. Redd growled in anger at Emily's refusal. "Don't fuck with me, Emily," he said. "Remember, you are under contract with me. You can get back to me, and I will erase everything that has happened to you. I will make you forget the family that never loved you, the college that never accepted you, and the people who doubted you. But if you reject me, say 'no' and turn your back on me, I will make your life a living Hell. You will be hated and jeered at by everyone around you in the town where you live. It's your choice, Emily. What's it gonna be?"

Emily no longer wanted to hear Mr. Redd's demands. "Sorry," she said. "But the answer is 'No.' Find yourself a new sex partner." She hung up the phone and went back to sleep. She wanted to go back to her old life. But Mr. Redd wasn't going to let her. He wanted revenge.

Emily and The Devil

Over the next few days, Emily attempted to return to her everyday life, but it soon began to sour. Her parents became furious after seeing the pictures on the internet. Emily realized that she was seen as a threat by every student on campus. There was even a news report about Emily and her scandalous video on TV. Everyone in town saw her and began to call her names. Preachers and parents called Emily "The Whore of Hades." Emily became more frightened than before. She had to get home before things got out of control.

As Emily arrived at her house, she saw her phone with 78 voice messages left on the answering machine. She played one of them. The voice message was from Mr. Redd, who called her 78 times. Emily was mortified to hear each message Mr. Redd had left for her. She tried to erase every one of them before her parents came home. The last message was a threatening recording of Mr. Redd in a deep, sinister-sounding voice. "Emily," he said. "This is your last chance! You must return to me, or I will send you to Hell!" Emily unplugged the telephone and went upstairs to her room.

Nine days later, Emily arrived at Halo University. She saw the college students on campus and approached them. "Hi," she said. But the students didn't look happy to see her. They looked disgusted.

"You slept with Mr. Redd in his penthouse," one of the students said. Emily thought he was kidding. But he wasn't. Then, another student said the same thing. More students approached her angrily, wanting answers about Mr. Redd from her. They were turning feral, like wild animals stalking their prey. Emily asked what was wrong with them. Just then, she sees Nicole with an angry mob behind her.

"THERE SHE IS," she shouted. "There's the little gold digger! SHE HAD SEX WITH MR. REDD!!"

Emily saw Nicole and the others coming towards her. She felt threatened by how feral they had all become. "What's going on here?" Emily shouted.

Nicole stepped forward, holding a sign that read: "Emily Richards Must Die!" in big, bold red letters. "We're getting rid of you, Richards," she said. "You belong in Hell with this piece of filth you're displaying! **GET HER!!**"

Emily screamed at the sight of the angry mob. In a state of fear, Emily quickly ran away. She needed to hide somewhere. Without being seen, Emily quietly made her way inside.

She was out of breath as she raced down the hallway. She needed to stop. Just then, Mr. Redd's voice came over the intercom, calling to Emily in a low, seductive tone. "Emily," he said. "I know you can't resist me. I want you to be with me. You are my little submissive. Don't resist your sexual urges. Come to me, my naughty little bitch." Emily tried to cover her ears to block out his words. But she couldn't stop the trembling in her body.

Emily ran into the bathroom to escape his voice. Again, she heard him calling out to her. "You can't run away from me," he said. "I know what lurks in your lustful heart. You have deep desires for more sex. I can feel it in your heart. Just come back to me and be mine."

Emily was starting to freak out. She looked in the mirror but found herself in the arms of Mr. Redd. Emily turned red at the sight of Mr. Redd touching her body and kissing her. She screamed and tried to turn away, but she fell to her knees, breathing heavily in panic. She couldn't take it anymore. It was too much for her to handle.

She rushed out of the bathroom to escape hearing his voice. But then, things got worse. Dean Woodrow called Emily to report to his office. So she did. Emily came to the Dean's office. Dean Woodrow was angry at Emily for posting the video on the computer.

"I am disgusted with you," he shouted. "You have no right to post this debauchery on the internet!" Emily was breathless as she attempted to explain. However, Dean Woodrow refused to listen to her. "You are expelled from Halo University," he yelled. "**GET OUT!!**"

Emily gasped. "Expelled?" she said. It was true. Emily got expelled from Halo University. She was no longer the popular girl on campus. All the students hate her. As Emily left the Dean's office, Nicole and the student body on campus chased after her. They shouted, "Go to Hell, Emily Richards!" while throwing rotten eggs and tomatoes at her in disgust. Emily ran down the street, avoiding the angry mob that wanted her removed from town permanently.

Later that afternoon, Emily came home. But as she came, she discovered that her home was now for sale. Her parents and her older brother are moving out. She saw a moving truck carrying all her stuff out of the house. Emily tried to stop them, but the movers told her that all her belongings had been donated to charity. Emily was outraged. Just then, she saw her mother and father. They didn't look happy to see her at all. "What's going on?" she asked.

Her parents gave her a disapproving look. "We're leaving you," Mr. Richards said.

"Leaving?" said Emily. "Why are you leaving?"

Mrs. Richards told Emily how they got a call from Mr. Redd about the video on the internet. They were angry with Emily. "You had sex with Mr. Redd," said Mr. Richards. "You left home without telling us, you had sex with a stranger, and you posted dirty videos of yourself onto social media."

Emily was surprised. Her parents were aware of the video on the internet. "We also received a call from the Dean stating that you were expelled from Halo University," said Mr. Richards. "Due to a video on the internet, we are extremely disappointed in you, Emily Richards!"

Emily wanted to tell him about the video on every computer on campus. "I can explain," she said. "Mr. Redd posted that video to blackmail me into returning to him." But her parents wouldn't listen. They never want to hear another word from Emily about Mr. Redd.

"We told you to end your relationship with him," Mr. Richards said. "But you didn't listen! We warned you not to date this man, and instead, you became a porn star with this filth on the computer!" Mr. Richards took his bags and loaded the van with Mrs. Richards and Marcus. They started to leave the house with all their baggage. Emily tried to stop them from leaving, but they pushed her aside, too upset with her for breaking their promise. Emily explained that she did try to end her relationship with Mr. Redd. But Emily received a spanking from him in his penthouse.

"He threatened to harm me if I don't do what he says," she said.

Mr. Richards told Emily to stop talking, having had enough of her. "We don't want to hear more about Mr. Redd," he said. "We don't want you in this family anymore! Consider yourself disowned!"

Emily gasped. She was no longer in the family. Emily was shocked to hear this. "I'm not in the family anymore?" she asked.

"No," her parents said.

"I'm ashamed to call you my daughter," Mrs. Richards said. Her parents turned away from Emily as they got into the van. Marcus approached her with a look of disappointment. He slapped her in the face bitterly.

"I hope you're proud of yourself, Emily," he said. "Do you know how embarrassing it is to have a sister who acts like a slut? Well, let me tell you. It's **VERY** embarrassing."

Emily and The Devil

Emily was devastated to hear her brother call her a slut to her face. Her parents left her alone and got into their Chevy van. They never said goodbye to her and drove off without looking back. Emily was devastated. Her parents had disowned her from the family. Sadly, Emily went inside the house and closed the door.

Emily sat alone in her empty bedroom, feeling the weight of loneliness pressing down on her. She cried in bed about losing her parents. She was feeling completely miserable.

# Chapter 10

That night, Emily sat alone in her empty house. The walls were bare, and the rooms were empty. She didn't want to be alone. So she got up from the floor and got dressed. Emily grabbed her bags and left the house. She turned around to see it one last time before she left. She walked down the street alone as she entered Downtown Halo Town. She could see the posters on every building calling for Emily's removal from town. Emily lowered her head in shame until she came upon a bus stop. There was no one around except for a flickering streetlight above her. Emily didn't take the bus. She called for a taxi instead. The cab pulled up, and Emily stepped inside. She told the driver to take her to a motel to stay for the night. The cab drove to a motel in town as the sun set over the horizon.

The motel was small with neon signs that flickered and buzzed dimly. As they arrived, Emily got out of the cab and went inside the motel. She called the motel desk clerk and requested a room for the night. The desk clerk gave her the key and showed her the door. Emily sadly made her way to her motel room upstairs. The room was small and a little dirty. It reminded her of her older brother's room. She put down her bags and sat down on the bed. The bed felt like her old bed back home before her parents took it away when they moved. Emily lay down and looked at the ceiling. The paint on the walls was chipped and peeling from old age. Emily was now the most hated person in Halo Town. Her family had moved out, and her belongings were gone. She was about to go to sleep with the sadness on her mind.

Suddenly, the motel telephone was ringing. Emily answered. "Hello," she said.

"Have you made your decision, Miss Emily?" Mr. Redd asked on the phone.

Emily gasped. "How did you get this number?" she asked.

But Mr. Redd interrupted her. "I want to know if you have made your decision," he said.

Emily broke down in tears. "What decision?" she asked.

"To come back to me and be mine," Mr. Redd said. Emily shook her head in disagreement.

"I can't," she said. "I don't want to come back to you."

Mr. Redd laughed. "But I miss you, babe," he said. "I need you to come back to me. Don't keep me waiting." Emily wanted to reject his phone call. But she couldn't. When she heard Mr. Redd's growl on the phone, she felt a slight sense of fear. "Let me remind you of the contract," Mr. Redd said. "I will have to send you to hell if you don't return to me!"

So, Emily reluctantly agreed to give him a visit. She left the motel and called a taxi. The taxi pulled up outside the motel, and Emily got inside. "Mr. Redd's penthouse, please," she told the driver. The cab pulled away, leaving Halo Town. Emily looked out the window as the lights of Halo Town began to disappear in the distance. She sighed as she lay down in the back seat of the taxi as it drove into Diablo City in the dead of night.

Twenty minutes later, the taxi arrived at Diablo City, and Emily returned to Mr. Redd's penthouse. She wanted to talk to him about what had happened over the past nine days since she left him. She got out of the taxi and headed inside the building. Making her way to the elevator, Emily stepped inside as the elevator began to rise. As soon as she entered, she saw Mr. Redd sitting at the piano bench. He was playing a sad-sounding sonata. Emily approached him and tapped on the lid. Mr. Redd stopped playing and looked up at her. "I knew you would come back," he said. "I've missed you."

But Emily wasn't happy. "I don't know what you did," she said. "But whatever it is, you'd better undo it." Mr. Redd didn't know what she was talking about.

"What's the matter?" he asked.

Emily told him again. "I want you to undo what you did to these people," she said firmly.

Mr. Redd, growing angry, stood up from his piano bench and approached Emily. "I don't know what you're talking about," he said.

Emily began to tell him what happened. "You posted a video on the internet," she said. "I got expelled from Halo University because of that video you sent me, everyone called me a whore, and my whole family left me because I ignored their warnings about my relationship with you."

Mr. Redd felt offended by Emily's words. He wanted to hit her, but he didn't. "Listen to me," he said. "You said you wanted to be with me forever, and I granted that wish. After all, I had planned this whole thing from the start."

Emily gasped. "What do you mean?" she asked.

Mr. Redd told her about the picture and the video online. "I posted the video of us on every computer as a setup to make you come back to me in my penthouse," he said. "The picture I sent to your college added more to the drama. And I called your parents and told them about your little display in the playroom. Does that answer your question, my little sex puppet?"

Emily was furious. Everything Mr. Redd did to her was a setup to get her to return to him, which would also explain why all the students turned against her in an angry mob. "You did all of this to get me to return to you?" she asked.

Mr. Redd smiled with a wicked grin. "Exactly," he said. "Everything I have done was all for you, baby."

"But why?" Emily asked.

Mr. Redd's expression changed. "You were the one who left me," he said. "You said you wanted to end our relationship. You called me a sadist, and I find that offensive. Well, I wasn't going to let you out of my sight. I want you to stay with me." Mr. Redd grabbed Emily's arm in a blistering grip.

"Let go of me," Emily said. Mr. Redd didn't want to let her go.

"You thought you could escape from me by breaking up with me," he said. "But you're wrong. I own you, Emily. Your soul, as well as your body, belongs to me for eternity." Mr. Redd picked up Emily, threw her over his arms, and brought her into his playroom. He sat her down on the whipping bench with an angry gesture. Emily looked up at him as his eyes turned red. A sneer curled on his lip. He was furious at her. "You know what I'm gonna do to you," he said. He ordered her to stand up and bend over on the bench.

"What are you going to do?" asked Emily.

"I'm gonna spank you 10 times," replied Mr. Redd in a strict, growling voice. "And you will count them for me." He lifted her skirt and pulled down her panties, exposing her buttocks. "You will not move from this spot as I spank you," he said.

Emily's heart was pounding with fear. Mr. Redd was about to spank her in his playroom. He took his whip and began to whip her on the buttocks 10 times. The sharp hits made Emily cry out in pain. As Mr. Redd whipped her, Emily counted the hits. "One, Two, Three, Four, Five, Six, Seven, Eight, Nine, Ten," she said. When he finished, he grabbed Emily by her neck and pulled her towards his face.

Emily's eyes filled with tears. "You said you would be less aggressive with me," she said. "You promised."

Mr. Redd frowned at her. "I lied," he said. "I lied about keeping my promise to you. You were right. I'm not a gentleman. I *AM* a sadist."

Emily gasped. Mr. Redd was not a gentleman. He was, in truth, a sadist. "I will do it again if you refuse my demands again," Mr. Redd said. "Do you understand, Emily?" Emily whimpered in tears. But answered his question.

"Yes, Sir," she said.

Mr. Redd spanked Emily again, which left her to burst into tears. Then, he grabbed Emily by her neck in a blistering grip. "This is your home now," he said. "And you will stay here forever. From now on, you will follow all my instructions. When I say, 'Come,' you say, 'Yes, Sir.' When I say, 'Meet me in my playroom,' you say, 'Yes, Sir." When I say, "You will wear the black mini-dress for me," you say, "Yes, Sir." And when I say, "You will have sex with me," you say, "Yes, Sir." Do you understand?"

Emily's breath raced as she noticed how dominant and aggressive Mr. Redd had become to her. It left her speechless without an answer. Mr. Redd frowned as he forced her to answer to him. "I asked if you understood," he said. Emily swallowed in fear as she replied.

"Yes, Sir," she said.

He put down the whip and helped Emily put her panties back on. Suddenly, he grabbed her neck and leaned towards Emily's ear. "Once you go red, you can never go back," said Mr. Redd. "There's no Prince Charming in this fairytale, Princess. There's only the Beast. There is no God, no Heaven, no mercy." Emily's breath shortened when she heard Mr. Redd's words as if they were a spell on her by just talking. "Forget about family," he added. "Forget about college. Forget about Halo Town. Forget about Freedom. You're mine, Emily Richards." Emily felt scared. She was so frightened that she fainted in his arms. Mr. Redd let go of her neck and took Emily to his bedroom for the remainder of the evening.

In the middle of the night, Emily lay in bed with Mr. Redd. She got out of bed and walked over to the balcony, gazing out at the city skyline with tears in her eyes. Not even the glow of the city lights would make her feel better. Her heart sank inside her chest at the mistake she had made. Now that she was no longer a student at Halo University and her parents were gone, she had no choice but to stay with Mr. Redd. Emily knew she should have listened to her parents and heeded their warnings about him, but she didn't. It was all her fault. She has lost everything.

The next day, Emily woke feeling sad about losing her parents and getting expelled from Halo University. She looked around the bedroom and found that Mr. Redd wasn't there. She left Mr. Redd's bedroom and found him at the piano. When Mr. Redd turned around, he saw that Emily was awake and dressed.

"Good morning," he said. It's so lovely to see you ready."

Emily looked at Mr. Redd and asked, "Ready for what?"

Mr. Redd got up from his piano bench and explained to her that he was taking her out to breakfast this morning. "I made reservations at Chez Michael's Bistro," he said. "Come. My limo is waiting." Mr. Redd took Emily's arm and brought her to his limo outside.

A few minutes later, they arrived at a fancy, lavish Bistro restaurant in Downtown Diablo City called Chez Michael's Bistro, located in the Hadestown District, a neighborhood with its own radio station. Mr. Redd ordered two plates for Emily and himself. The waiter brought out their plates, and they began to eat. Emily felt a little sad. She didn't want to eat anything. Mr. Redd looked at her and gave her the plate. "You need to eat," he said. "You don't want to go hungry forever, do you?"

Emily looked at her plate and frowned.

Mr. Redd asked, "Aren't you hungry?"

Emily looked up at him and shook her head. "No," she said. "I'm feeling sick."

Mr. Redd didn't believe her. He told her to eat before her breakfast got cold. But Emily didn't want to eat. She couldn't stop thinking about the night she spent in the playroom. "I'm not hungry," she said. "I want to go home."

Mr. Redd frowned at Emily. He didn't like how she was acting towards him. "Emily," said Mr. Redd. "I am not a patient man. Now, eat before I have to punish you." Emily felt threatened by his words. Mr. Redd wasn't going to wait for Emily to finish her breakfast. So, he got up from his table and brought Emily to the back of the restaurant to give her a disciplinary talk.

"Where are you taking me?" Emily asked. Mr. Redd said nothing. He led her to an empty room in the back corner and closed the door behind them.

"You know the penalty for disobeying my demands," he said in a strict tone. "Now, bend over." Emily bent over, allowing Mr. Redd to give her full access to her butt. Mr. Redd pulled out his belt and began to spank her 6 times. When he finished, he brought Emily up and looked at her. "Will you eat breakfast without acting like a brat?" he asked.

Emily nodded her head in response. "Yes, Sir," she said. The two left the back corner and returned to their table together. Emily sat down to finish her breakfast.

However, her butt felt sore from the spanking. Perhaps her parents were right about Mr. Redd being a danger. She began to eat her breakfast while Mr. Redd watched. He sat and watched Emily without touching his plate. He was more interested in seeing Emily be obedient towards him. Tears fell from Emily's eyes as she tried to eat. But she still felt the stinging pain from her butt, like a burning whip leaving marks on her skin.

After breakfast, they left the restaurant and entered Mr. Redd's limousine. They returned to Mr. Redd's penthouse for the rest of the day. When they arrived, Mr. Redd brought Emily into his playroom and handcuffed her to the bench. He began to give her 10 more spankings for the mistakes she made. When Mr. Redd finished spanking her, he brought her face towards him with force. He began to remove her clothes. Then, he brought her to an X-cross next to the bed. He cuffed both her wrists and ankles to the X-cross and began to have sex with her in his playroom.

Emily felt hurt by how Mr. Redd was penetrating her harshly. Every thrust he gave her was more painful than the last time he did it to her in his bedroom. "Please, stop," Emily begged.

But Mr. Redd hits her even harder. "Never," he said. "You're mine to control, Emily. Your soul belongs to me." He continued to penetrate her with more brutal hits on the X-cross than it hit the wall. Mr. Redd growled and groaned from the pleasure and dominant power he was experiencing. The sounds merged with Emily's whimpered cries as he reached his ultimate climax. Finally, Mr. Redd let out a roar of orgasm. The walls shook from his loud noise, like a beast was about to break free from its bounds. When it was over, Mr. Redd uncuffed Emily from the X-cross and brought her to his bedroom for the remainder of the night.

As they entered, Emily walked over to the window. The night sky had no stars or a moon. The only lights were from the city below. Just then, Mr. Redd came up from behind Emily and grabbed her arms. "Come to bed," he said. "You'll need to get some rest." But Emily didn't want to sleep in the same bed as him, and she was still upset about how he had treated her. Mr. Redd brought Emily away from the window and sat her on the bed. Then, he removed his bathrobe and tossed it aside. He joined her in bed, and the two went to sleep.

The next day, Emily woke up and got out of bed. She dressed herself in clean clothes. Emily began to leave the bedroom and looked around the penthouse alone. "Hello," she said. "Anyone here?"

Soon, Emily came upon a door in the dining room. Burning with curiosity, Emily approached the door. When she opened the door, she saw an office inside. Emily carefully went in and found a notebook on Mr. Redd's desk. It had Mr. Redd's name on it. She picked up the notebook and went through the pages. Each page listed the previous women Mr. Redd had brought into his playroom. It shocked Emily to the core with fear. All these women of the past were Mr. Redd's sex submissives who sold their souls to him for pleasure and luxury. When she saw her name on the page, she screamed and dropped the notebook to the ground.

Emily grabbed her chest and backed away from the notebook. Emily breathed heavily, seeing her name in Mr. Redd's notebook. "It can't be," she said. Suddenly, she heard the door opening. Mr. Redd saw Emily on the floor, breathing rapidly in panic. Mr. Redd gave her a look.

"What are you doing in my office?" he asked. Emily was startled. His appearance was intimidating when he entered.

"Mr. Redd," she said.

"What is this?" Mr. Redd frowned at Emily. "You should know better than to go into my office," he said. "This is for my business use only. "

He walked up to Emily. But she backed away from him. "Don't come any closer," Emily said. "You are a pimp!"

Mr. Redd frowned at Emily. "Why do you say that?" he asked.

"I saw the list of previous women in your notebook," Emily replied. She points at the notebook on the floor. "Who are these women, and why are they on your list?" she yelled. "More importantly, why is my name on your list?"

Mr. Redd noticed the notebook and picked it up. Then, he looked at Emily with the same burning red eyes. "Naughty Emily," he said. "You've been very naughty indeed. Daddy's going to have to teach you a lesson."

But Emily stepped back from him, standing against the wall. "Stay away," she said. "Who do you think you are?"

Mr. Redd picked up the notebook and put it back on the desk. "I'm your master," he said. "And you should know better than to sneak into my office without permission. Now stop avoiding me and come here." Emily didn't want to come near him. She was both scared and angry at the same time.

"What kind of man are you?" she asked. Mr. Redd's eyes changed color at Emily's question.

"Do you want to know the truth about me?" Mr. Redd asked. Emily demanded to know what kind of man he was. So Mr. Redd told her the truth about himself.

"You've heard the saying, speak of the devil?" he asked.

Emily looked at him, confused. "No, I don't," she said.

"Well, that's who I am," said Mr. Redd. Emily wasn't sure what he was talking about.

"Who are you?" she asked.

Mr. Redd gave her a wickedly sinful grin. "I'm the devil," he said in a low, deep voice. Emily was startled to hear him say those words to her. She pulled away from his touch and stepped back.

"You're the devil?" she asked.

"I *AM* the devil," said Mr. Redd. "I am Lucifer, Satan, Beelzebub, the Prince of Darkness!! Well, King of Darkness." Emily thought this was a joke.

"You're weird," she said.

"What exactly do you mean?" Mr. Redd didn't like to be mocked by Emily's insults. "Perhaps no one told you about me," he said. "I come from Hell. The realm of evil and darkness where I rule. I go by many names, people call me."

Emily looked at him strangely. "You're from Hell?" she asked.

"Yes," Mr. Redd said. "I collect the souls of humans whom I tempt into selling them to me for what they want. What I give them in return is an eternity in Hell. Just like what I gave you, Emily."

Emily still didn't believe him. She thought he was reciting lines from a movie or a play. "But you don't look anything like the devil," she said in disbelief.

Mr. Redd grinned at her. "You're right," he said. "I could have appeared to you like this." With a snap of his fingers, he transformed into his devil form in front of Emily, much to her shock. He had red skin, a goatee beard, slick black hair, sharp horns, a tail, pointed ears, a cape, and a pitchfork in his left hand. "But that's for Halloween," he said.

Emily was shocked to see Mr. Redd in his devil form. "It's true," she said. "You are the devil." Mr. Redd returned to his human form and approached Emily.

"You see," he said. "Even the most gorgeous-looking man can turn out to be the villain." Emily felt betrayed. Mr. Redd was indeed the Devil in Disguise.

"Oh no," she said. "So it is true. I thought you were a man. But now I know that you're the devil."

Mr. Redd laughed at seeing Emily shaken from witnessing his image. "I also lied about my age," he said. "I'm not 26 years old. I'm much older than that. "I'm 6,000 years old."

Emily gasped at hearing how old Mr. Redd was. "6,000 years old?" she asked. "Oh my God!" Mr. Redd stomped his foot down hard to tell Emily never to mention God in his presence.

"You have seen my true nature," he said. "Now, you shall stay here forever." Emily felt her heartbeat increasing inside her chest at the sight of Mr. Redd's demon form.

"If you're the devil," she said. "Why did you want me to stay with you?"

Mr. Redd slammed his hands up against the wall. "I have been watching you from a distance," he said. "I wanted you to sell your soul to me, so I ensured it worked. I manipulated you into giving yourself to me with sex. I made you submit to me with the wine I gave you. And now you are my slave to bend to my whim. You didn't notice me, but I've been there since you said you'd give anything for a luxurious life."

Emily recalled the day she was late for college. But she never noticed Mr. Redd spying on her from a distance. Realizing this, Emily was shocked. "You were spying on me?" she asked.

"Exactly," said Mr. Redd with a grin. "I bribed you into giving your soul to me. You said you'd give anything for a luxurious lifestyle, and I heard your wish. Seeing how miserable you were, I knew you would be perfect to be my Submissive sex slave."

Emily was shocked to hear Mr. Redd say he'd been watching her. She recalled the wine he made her drink, which made her do all the naughty things he intended her to do for him, including dancing with him at the nightclub.

"You turned me into a whore," she growled. "That explains why I got kicked out of college and why my family abandoned me! It was YOU!!"

Mr. Redd approached Emily quickly. "Don't be so frightened," he said. "You should be glad I made you what you are." Mr. Redd leaned over to Emily and attempted to kiss her on the lips. But Emily slapped Mr. Redd in the face with anger.

"GET AWAY FROM ME!" she yelled. "I don't want to be near someone who's a devil!"

Mr. Redd growled at Emily for slapping him in the face. His eyes begin to turn red. "You were the one who said you wanted a life of luxury," he growled. "I gave it to you. Without me, you'd be back with your pathetic life and be miserable forever."

Still afraid, Emily told Mr. Redd she didn't want to be his submissive slave forever. "I want my old life back," she said. "I want you to return me to Halo Town immediately!"

But Mr. Redd didn't listen. "We had a deal," he said. "You signed the contract. You belong to me forever!" He showed Emily the contract she signed just as before. Emily looked at her name in red ink. Mr. Redd revealed to Emily that the red ink from her pen was blood. Emily signed her name in blood. She was outraged.

"You tricked me," Emily said. Mr. Redd approached her and frowned. He pinned her to the wall and forced her to gaze into his eyes.

"Do I look like the kind of man who would trick you?" he asked. Emily looked into his eyes as they turned red before her. Emily panicked in fear. She felt hurt to realize Mr. Redd's plan. She broke free from his pinning, picked up a vase, and threw it at him in a fit of anger.

"You dirty, rotten **BASTARD**!" she said. "**I HATE YOU!!**"

Mr. Redd's eyes soon turned red, and he became angry upon hearing Emily call him a bastard, prompting him to throw a vase at her. He approached Emily and slapped her in the face. "Love me or hate me, you are mine forever," he said.

Emily was furious about her mistake and wanted to undo what had happened. "I wish I hadn't signed the contract," she said.

Mr. Redd grabbed Emily's face in anger. "You can't return on a deal," he said. "Your soul belongs to me once you sign the contract in blood. Also, you owe me a new vase." Mr. Redd grabbed Emily's arm and took her to his playroom. He closed the door behind him and walked up to Emily. Mr. Redd pulled a thick, leather bullwhip and cracked it across Emily's back. He unzipped his pants and inserted his hand.

Then, Mr. Redd pulled out his cock and commanded Emily to crawl to him. "Come to me," he said. Emily shook her head in protest. Mr. Redd grew angry and cracked his whip hard. "If you don't come to me, I will have to spank you," he said. She didn't want to receive another spanking from Mr. Redd. But Mr. Redd told her to crawl to him. So he wrapped the whip around Emily's neck and pulled her towards his crotch. Emily's face met with Mr. Redd's massive cock. She looked up at him with wide eyes as Mr. Redd demanded that she suck his manhood while he spanked her butt. So, she did as Mr. Redd ordered. Emily gave Mr. Redd a blowjob as she received her spanking from him.

Emily's mouth stretched to the size of his enlarged member as Mr. Redd moaned and groaned in the playroom. Mr. Redd threw his head back in arousal from Emily's mouth on his cock. As he moaned, he spanked Emily's butt with his whip sharply, making Emily cry out in pain. Her cries were muffled by Mr. Redd's manhood in her mouth as it reached deeper inside. Mr. Redd thrusted his hips harder as his eyes rolled to the back of his head. His eyes were filled with pleasure as he reached his orgasm. Mr. Redd told Emily to keep sucking him while he spanked her more. Emily was choking until she was about to pass out, but she kept sucking him no matter what. Finally, Mr. Redd released his orgasm inside Emily's mouth.

After he finished, Mr. Redd pulled Emily away from his cock and lifted her to meet his gaze. But Emily stepped back from him, still feeling the salty cum in her mouth. She coughed out the taste in disgust. It was nasty for her to swallow a man's bodily fluid. "Why did you do that?" she asked.

Mr. Redd wrapped the whip around Emily's waist and pulled her to him. "I just wanted to teach you a lesson," he said. He took Emily to the bondage bed and removed her clothes until she was naked. Mr. Redd wrapped his arm around her waist and leaned in to kiss her. Only it wasn't a kiss. It was a bite on her neck that he was giving her. "I told you," he said. "You cannot resist me. You can never leave me."

He turned Emily over and positioned himself on top of her body. Mr. Redd inserted his cock inside Emily once again and began to have sex while she cried in pain. Mr. Redd gave Emily brutal penetrations in his bed until he orgasmed again. He removed himself from Emily and brought her to the floor. Then, he began to leave the playroom and locked Emily inside.

"You may come out when you've learned to be a good Submissive toy," Mr. Redd said. Emily ran to the door and cried to let Mr. Redd free her. She pounded on the door and screamed in anger.

"Let me out!" she yelled. "Let me out!" But Mr. Redd never came back.

Emily stopped pounding on the door and fell to the floor, bursting into tears. "I can't believe Mr. Redd is the devil," she said. "What have I done? What should I do?"

Emily and The Devil

That evening, Emily awoke after feeling a little better. However, she still felt trapped in Mr. Redd's playroom, which had become a prison for her. Emily wanted to escape while she still had a life to live, but Mr. Redd had locked the playroom door from the outside. She felt like a prisoner to Mr. Redd, and what was worse, Emily was shocked to discover that Mr. Redd was the Devil. The man she had fallen in love with was a demon from hell. Emily needed help. She went into the closet to find another key that could open the door to free her. However, as Emily went through each drawer, Emily couldn't find anything to open the door. Just then, she could hear the door open. Emily quickly got out of the closet and closed the door.

As the door opened, Emily could see Mr. Redd enter the playroom. "There's my good submissive toy," he said. Mr. Redd approached Emily and picked her up. He took her out of the playroom and closed the door behind him. They entered his bedroom, and Mr. Redd removed his leather pants while Emily lay on the bed. He joined Emily in bed naked and lay down beside her with his arms wrapped around her body, hoping she would not escape from him. Emily curled up in a fetal position as she started to cry from the stinging pain of the bullwhip on her body. She felt guilty about making a deal with the devil. As Emily slept, Mr. Redd heard her heart beating in her chest. His hand grabbed her left breast and silenced her heart.

For the next two weeks, Emily continued living with Mr. Redd in his penthouse as his sex slave in their non-romantic sexual relationship. She went everywhere with him, but not to the romantic places he had promised to take her. Mr. Redd took Emily to the Devil's Playground in the downtown area, where they purchased BDSM items from adult stores and returned to his penthouse for their nights of BDSM sex in the playroom.

But she soon became bored and tired of her luxurious lifestyle. The life that she wanted was not what she had expected. Emily's luxurious life had been a trap set up by Mr. Redd to hold her captive as his sex slave. What was even worse, Mr. Redd didn't want to let her go. She belonged to him forever. She tried to end her relationship with him, but couldn't think of a way to do so. She got so swept up in all the glamour of his lavish lifestyle that she had forgotten everything about her home in Halo Town and the people around her.

# Chapter 11

Two weeks later, Emily woke up at the first sunrise outside the window. She turned to the other side and saw Mr. Redd sleeping beside her on his bed. She didn't want to wake him, so Emily quietly sneaked out of bed and left the penthouse. However, as she was about to head out, Mr. Redd woke up and stopped her.

"Going somewhere?" he said. Emily turned around. She saw Mr. Redd sitting up in his bed, completely naked. "You're not leaving me, are you?" Mr. Redd asked.

Emily was still upset with him for spanking her and locking her in his playroom the previous night. "I don't want any more of your dominance," she said.

Mr. Redd pulled out his hand and commanded her to come to him. "Come here," he said in a low-toned voice. Emily returned to his bed and sat down. Then, Mr. Redd straddled her, pinning her wrists to his bed.

Emily looked into his eyes, but was frightened at how red they looked. He was still demanding that Emily be his submissive forever. "Look at me, baby," said Mr. Redd. "Look into my eyes."

Mr. Redd began to have sex with her in his bed to teach her a lesson. Only this time, his way of having sex with her was giving her pain rather than pleasure. Then, after he finished, he removed himself from Emily and began to take a shower. Emily left the balcony alone to take in the city view, feeling fatigued and heavy-hearted. But not even the view of Diablo City would cheer her up. The memories of her home were gone. All the sweetness had turned sour for her. She returned to the living room, where Mr. Redd stood before her, wearing a towel around his waist.

"I hope you slept well," he said. Emily looked up at him, sadness and anger etched in her eyes. Mr. Redd approached her and wrapped his arms around her waist. "I think you have massive potential," he said. "If you're facing an eternity in hell, let me tell you, having a friend like me wouldn't hurt. So you think about that." After he let go of her face, he began to get dressed for work.

A few minutes later, Mr. Redd emerged from the bedroom, dressed in his red suit. "Time to go," he said.

Mr. Redd wanted Emily to come with him. "Why do I have to go to work with you?" Emily asked.

Mr. Redd gave her a nasty look as he walked towards her. "Because I said so," Mr. Redd said. But she didn't want to go to work. Mr. Redd took out his belt and whipped her with it. "Do I need to remind you again?" he asked. "Am I going to have to spank you?"

Emily shook her head in response. "No, sir," she said. Emily had no choice but to accompany him to work.

"Good," said Mr. Redd. "Get dressed." So Emily dressed in her red suit and joined Mr. Redd to work. They left the penthouse and got into Mr. Redd's limousine outside.

Emily and The Devil

At Redd Enterprises, Mr. Redd was holding a meeting in the conference room, and Emily sat next to him for support. But deep down, she began to despise him for what he did to her last night. Mr. Redd noticed Emily looking away and whipped her buttocks sharply. He wanted her to pay attention. Emily tried to hold back the tears in her eyes, but it was no good. The pain was too much for her to take. After the meeting, Mr. Redd took Emily out of the conference room. He noticed Emily frowning and looking at the floor. Mr. Redd grabbed the back of her head and pulled her up towards the front. "You mustn't lower your head like that in my presence," he said in her ear. He let go of her hair and took her by the arm as they walked down the hallway.

Later that same day, Mr. Redd presented the economy's expansion to a group of visiting chief executive officers from various industry companies in Diablo City. Emily was the representative to Mr. Redd. While he gave his speech to the board of CEOs, Emily looked out the window and sighed, becoming bored. But Mr. Redd pinched her cheek to get her to pay attention. His words throughout the speech drew the CEO's attention to him like a hypnotic spell. After the presentation, the Chief Executive Officers shook Mr. Redd's hand and left the building. As soon as they went, Mr. Redd brought Emily to his office.

When they arrived, Mr. Redd looked at Emily, who had her head down the entire time. "Don't look so sad," he said. "I know what you need. You need me to fuck you right here in this office."

So, without warning, Mr. Redd lifted Emily onto his desk. Grabbing her upper thighs, he forced her legs apart and made his way between them. His actions mortified Emily. She wanted to get up, but she couldn't. The weight of his hips was weighing her down with so much pressure that it made it impossible for her to move. Mr. Redd unzipped his pants and pulled out his cock as he was about to give her some brutal penetration on his desk.

Emily didn't want to allow him to give her pleasure. She was too scared. He grabbed the back of her head and pulled her to his lips. But as he was about to kiss her, Emily pushed him away from her and stood up from his desk.

"What the fuck?" Mr. Redd shouted. Emily kicked Mr. Redd in the leg in anger. She ran out of his office in fear, knowing she could escape him as quickly as possible. Mr. Redd tried to stop her, but she was already gone. "Emily, come back," he yelled. He went after her to the elevator. However, the elevator doors closed before Mr. Redd could stop her.

As Emily left the building, she ran to find someone to help her. She headed to a police station downtown on the corner to seek help. Emily approached the bench where a police chief sat.

"Excuse me," she said.

The police chief looked up at her. "Can I help you?" he said.

Emily began to speak. "I need you to arrest a sinister man," she said. "He's six feet tall, with black hair and red eyes."

The police chief instructed the others to initiate a citizen's arrest. "Name of the criminal?" he asked.

Emily told the police chief the criminal was Mr. Redd. The police chief stopped her suddenly. "You mean *THE* Mr. Redd of Redd Enterprises?" he asked.

"Yes," said Emily. The police chief asked her why he would want to arrest Mr. Redd. Emily explained to him about Mr. Redd. "He's the devil from Hell," she said. "He made me sell my soul to him to be his sex submissive. You have to save me from him. He's a Sadist, and he has a sex dungeon in his penthouse. He locks me in there every night, and he beats me in there."

The police chief looked at her and laughed. "That's the funniest thing I've heard," he said. "A man who thinks he's a devil? How pathetic."

But Emily was being serious. "Mr. Redd is the devil," she said. "I sold my soul to him for a life of luxury in exchange for being his sex slave!"

The police chief didn't believe her. "You don't have any proof," he said. "If he's the Devil, where are his horns and pitchfork?"

Emily didn't have a picture of Mr. Redd, but she explained the contract. "He has a contract in his office," she said. "He made me sign my name in blood. He collects the souls of other women to be his prisoners for his pleasure."

However, the police chief still didn't believe her. He thought she was crazy. So, he called two of his officers to take Emily outside. "Call us when there's a *REAL* crime," he said. Emily tried to get him to listen, but nothing seemed to work.

"You don't understand," she yelled. "He is the devil! You have to believe me!" She left the police station wholly devastated.

However, as she was leaving the police station, she saw Mr. Redd approaching her. "Why did you leave me?" he said.

Emily tried to run away, but Mr. Redd grabbed her by the arm in a blistering grip. "I said, why did you leave me?" he said. "Answer me!" Emily didn't answer his question. Mr. Redd picked her up and took her to his car. Emily kicked and screamed at him.

"Let me go," she shouted. But he didn't let her go. Mr. Redd put her in the back seat and got inside.

"You and I are going to discuss when we get home," he growled. Then, he drove her back to his penthouse to reason with her. Upon arriving, Mr. Redd carried her into the living room and threw her onto the couch with force. "Do you have any idea how worried you made me?" he said in a frustrated tone. "I could have lost you!"

Emily felt resentment towards the way he treated her. "Why were you trying to have sex with me in your office?" she asked. "What if someone came in and saw us together?"

Mr. Redd didn't care if someone walked in on them in his office. He was furious with Emily for running away from him at work. "You owe me an apology in my office this afternoon," he said. "Now you will pay for it."

Emily's eyes filled with tears of hatred from Mr. Redd's words. "Why do you do this to me?" she asked.

"Because it's who I am," said Mr. Redd. "I am the devil. I make the rules, and I expect them to be obeyed!"

Mr. Redd grabbed her by her wrists and brought her to his playroom again. He stripped Emily naked and put her on the bondage bed. He secured her hands and feet to the bedpost with leather straps to keep her from moving. Mr. Redd aggressively pursued Emily to make up for their moment in his office. Emily's body ached and burned from Mr. Redd's heavy thrusting. She was so frightened of his dominating nature that it made her cry again. Mr. Redd noticed Emily's tears and stopped his penetrating. Then, he brought her to the whipping bench and began to whip her butt 20 more times.

Next, he penetrated her from behind while he spanked her brutally. The stinging pain was leaving deep marks on Emily's body as Mr. Redd thrusted her more profoundly and more complexly. He exploded in an orgasm and removed himself from Emily. As he stood, he admired the view of Emily's body, which had red scars and marks, and smiled. Drops of blood were leaking from her skin, mixing with her tears. Then, he grabbed her by her hair and pulled her face towards him. "Never piss me off again," he growled. "You stay in here and think about what you did!" Mr. Redd locked Emily in his playroom as punishment for escaping him.

That evening, Mr. Redd returned to the playroom and brought Emily to his bedroom for the night. As they came into the bedroom, Emily looked at Mr. Redd with tears in her eyes. He was still angry with her for leaving his office earlier that day. "Why the fuck were you at a police station?" he asked.

Emily lowered her head to hide her face from him. "I tried to report you to the police," she said.

Mr. Redd smacked Emily in the face. "You were trying to report me to the police?" he asked. "Why would you do such a stupid thing like that?"

Emily grew angry at him for smacking her. "You were trying to have sex with me in your office," she said. "What were you thinking?"

Mr. Redd didn't like Emily's attitude towards him. "Maybe you forgot that I own you," he said. "So why don't you just forget your fucking attempt to escape from me! You belong here now!"

Emily slapped Mr. Redd in the face in anger. But Mr. Redd overpowered her and threw her onto the bed. "Don't ever hit me like that again," he said. "I am the dominant one here! You are the submissive! So don't fuck with me!"

Emily was so upset that she stormed out of Mr. Redd's bedroom. "Where are you going?" Mr. Redd asked.

"I'm going to sleep in the living room," Emily replied. "I can't sleep in the same bed with you." But Mr. Redd didn't want Emily to leave his bedroom. He blocked the door to keep her from leaving.

"You're not going anywhere," he said. "I'm incapable of leaving you alone. Now get the fuck to bed!" Emily was too tired to deal with Mr. Redd. So, she reluctantly went straight to bed. She got under the covers and fell asleep.

The next day, Emily woke up and got out of bed. She quietly got dressed and left Mr. Redd's bedroom without waking him. She entered the living room and picked up a phone book she had found, looking for an attorney on one of the pages. She called a few lawyers on the phone and asked questions about their experience with the "me too" movement. When she found the right lawyer, Emily was relieved. Her name was Tiana Webster, a female attorney with experience in the "Me Too" movement.

"Hello," said Tiana.

"My name is Emily Richards," said Emily. "I have a case I wish for you to take."

Tiana agreed and gave her the address to discuss the case. "Thank you," said Emily. When she saw the address, Emily quietly left the penthouse, not wanting Mr. Redd to know where she was. A few minutes later, she found herself walking alone in Diablo City.

Emily felt like a stranger to the people around her. She approached the law office to meet Tiana in person.

Inside, Emily explained to Tiana about her relationship with Mr. Redd. Tiana gasped at every word Emily said. She added that Mr. Redd was the Devil who made her sell her soul to him to be his submissive, and she wants to end her relationship. Tiana understood Emily and agreed to help her with the case. The two ladies made a compelling case and proceeded to the courthouse.

At the courthouse, Tiana approached the Judge and explained Emily's relationship with Mr. Redd. "My client, Ms. Emily Richards, is a good woman," she said. "She had a family and a life in a small town until she fell prey to a man named Mr. Redd, who manipulated her into selling her soul to him for a life of luxury. In return, he made her his submissive partner and performed harmful acts on her. He physically disciplined her, sexually harassed her, and threatened to harm her if she refused his demands."

The Judge looked at her oddly. "Say what?" he said.

Emily began to explain to the Judge about Mr. Redd. "He's the Devil, and he's a sadist," she said. "He made me his sex slave, and he does BDSM to me. He has a dungeon full of sex items he uses on me. That's why I need to sue him for domestic abuse."

It made the Judge upset. "I can't believe what I'm hearing," he said. Emily wanted to continue, but the Judge interrupted her. "Listen here," he said. "I did not become a judge to listen to some crazy bitch raving like a lunatic about some playboy sadist making a ditzy blonde like you be his little whore!"

Emily felt insulted to be called crazy by the Judge in a courthouse. "Please, listen to me," she said. However, the Judge, being corrupt, didn't want to hear another word from her.

"SHUT UP, you stupid bitch," he said. "I want you to get your ass out of my courtroom before I get mean!" Emily and Tiana lost the charge in utter defeat. Tiana was upset because she knew she had done the best job. "Find yourself a new lawyer," she said. "I quit." Emily and Tiana left the courtroom and went their separate ways. In frustration, Emily headed down the street. She was in trouble because she brought these charges against Mr. Redd.

Just then, she noticed Mr. Redd's limousine outside, just as it had been before, at the police station. The limo pulled up, and the door opened. Mr. Redd's driver stepped out of the limo and looked at Emily. "Mr. Redd requests that you return to him immediately," he said. But Emily didn't want to return to Mr. Redd; she was tired of his dominance over her. Unfortunately, the driver had no choice but to bring her into Mr. Redd's limo and drive her back to his penthouse without saying a word. As Emily returned to Mr. Redd's penthouse, the driver escorted her into the living room before leaving. Mr. Redd looked at Emily with fire in his eyes. He was angry with her for leaving his penthouse without his consent. "Where have you been?" he asked. Emily was terrified to see the anger in Mr. Redd's eyes.

Mr. Redd got up from his chair and walked up to Emily. "I asked you a question," he said. "I said, 'Where have you been?'"

Emily's eyes began to fill with tears, but she told him the truth about where she went. "I was at the courthouse in town," she said.

Mr. Redd was furious. "Why were you at a courthouse?" he asked.

Emily explained to Mr. Redd that she was trying to tell the judge about how aggressive he had been and wanted to sue him for abusing her.

Mr. Redd got angry at Emily. "You were going to sue me for keeping you in my penthouse?" he asked. Emily trembled at Mr. Redd's anger, unable to think of an excuse for why she was leaving him again. It only made Mr. Redd furious. He came up to her and grabbed her by the arm in a blistering grip.

Emily cried out in pain. "Let me go," she hollered. "You're hurting me!"

Mr. Redd brought her to his face and gritted his teeth in hatred. "I'll do more than just hurt you, my submissive, if you don't answer the fucking question," he hissed.

So Emily answered his question. "Yes," she said. "I was going to sue you for your aggressive behavior."

Mr. Redd slapped Emily in the face in anger, and she fell to the floor in tears. "OW!" cried Emily. "You hit me!" Emily's face was stinging red from the pain.

"I can do it again," Mr. Redd said. "Would you like that?"

But Emily didn't want to be hit again. "No," she yelled. "I won't like that!"

Mr. Redd stood over her, frowning. "Get up," he said. But Emily didn't want to. Her body was still aching from the pain. "Get up," Mr. Redd said again. Emily didn't move. He became very impatient with her. "**I SAID GET UP!**" he shouted.

Emily couldn't take any more of his dominance, pressuring her. "Mr. Redd, please," she said. "This is going too far."

Mr. Redd grabbed her face and pulled her towards him. "Not far enough," he said. "You forgot that I am your master. I do whatever I please to my submissive for my pleasure. You will enjoy it as much as I do. Because if you don't, you will burn in hell."

Emily felt threatened by Mr. Redd's words. She got mad at him and pulled away from his grip. "You, sadistic asshole," she yelled. "I'm not a toy for you to play with. I don't deserve this kind of mistreatment!!"

Mr. Redd slapped Emily again, and tears began to fall from her eyes. Mr. Redd was starting to get annoyed by Emily's resistance. He wasn't going to let her go. "Then I will make you suffer," he said. He grabbed her by the wrists and pinned her to the wall. Mr. Redd tightened his grip on her wrists until they hurt her so much, leaving Emily to cry. "Why do you resist me?" he said. Emily struggled to escape. His hands gripped her wrists tightly.

Mr. Redd brought Emily to his playroom and put her on the whipping bench. He pulled her skirt and panties down, exposing her butt. He began to whip her on her butt 20 times. Emily told him to stop. She couldn't take this anymore. "Let this be a warning to you, Emily!" he growled. "The next time you leave my place, I will send you to Hell bare naked!"

Poor Emily was left bleeding and crying from the pain she had received. "I don't want any more of this pain," Emily said. Mr. Redd smacked her in the face with his belt, and she fell to the floor in tears.

"Well, too bad," he said. "Your soul is mine." Mr. Redd locked her in his playroom and headed to his private gym for a workout.

"You *MONSTER*!" she yelled.

The next day, Emily left Mr. Redd's penthouse to clear her mind from having endless nights of Mr. Redd's dominance. As Emily walked down the street, she came across a nearby church and went inside. Emily thought that if she could speak to someone about Mr. Redd, they might be able to help her get out of her relationship with him. Just then, a preacher approached her. "What seems to be troubling you, my child?" he asked.

Emily looked at the preacher and stood up. "I need to speak to God," she said.

"That is through the power of prayer," the preacher said. But Emily didn't have time for a prayer.

"I need to speak to God in person," she said.

The preacher gave her a look and asked her a question. "Why do you need to speak to God?"

Emily explained to the preacher why she wanted to speak to God. "I need to get out of a non-romantic, sexual relationship," she said. "I sold my soul to the devil for a life of luxury, and he has made me his submissive prisoner in his penthouse."

The preacher was disgusted by Emily's words. He thought she was crazy. The preacher kicked her out of the church in anger. "Don't ever come here again, sinner," he yelled.

Emily tried to explain Mr. Redd to the preacher. However, he refused to listen to her. "You must listen to me," she yelled. But it was too late. The preacher told Emily to leave and closed the door.

Emily was upset. The church preacher couldn't help her get out of her deal with Mr. Redd. Sadly, Emily walked away from the church and down the street, feeling defeated. Tears started to form in her eyes as she brought her hands up to her face. "What do I do now?" she said. Emily's heart sank inside her. No one in the city could help her. Not the police, not the judge, not even the preacher. Emily was losing hope in herself. Emily returned to Mr. Redd's penthouse before the rain started to fall. However, it began to rain. Emily was feeling drenched and cold as the rain came down hard. Thunder and lightning roared in the sky. The sound frightened Emily, making her think of the roaring in Mr. Redd's voice.

When Emily returned to Mr. Redd's penthouse, she was soaking wet from the rain. She removed her wet clothes and put them in the hamper down the hallway. Next, she went into the bathroom and dried herself with a clean towel. She put on a bathrobe and went into the living room to watch TV until Mr. Redd came home. But she also considered what Mr. Redd would do to her if he came home. She didn't want to argue with him again. So, she kept quiet for the rest of the day.

That evening, Mr. Redd came home and found Emily sitting in the living room. He noticed the bathrobe she was wearing and thought that she had taken a shower for him to surprise him when he entered the room. He sniffed her body and purred with delight. "You smell nice," he said. Emily turned to face him but said nothing. Mr. Redd leaned closer to her and whispered in her ear. "I want you in my playroom in 10 minutes," he said. "I have a little something for you." Mr. Redd went into the bathroom to take a shower after a long, hard day at work. Emily got up from the couch and went to Mr. Redd's playroom. She removed her robe and tossed it aside. She came up to the bondage bed and got down on her knees, awaiting Mr. Redd's orders. A few minutes later, Mr. Redd entered the playroom wearing black leather pants and no shirt. He saw Emily on her knees, facing the bondage bed naked. Mr. Redd was pleased to see how obedient Emily was acting. But deep down, Emily was still thinking about the pain she would receive. "I await your pleasure, Master," she said calmly. Mr. Redd closed the door behind him and went over to his BDSM closet.

He pulled out a black restraint spreader bar with handcuffs, ankle cuffs, and a vibrator for Emily. He gestured for her to sit on the edge of the bondage bed and lift her legs. Next, he put the spreader bar on Emily's ankles. He secured her hands on the handcuffs, turned her over, and positioned her on the bed. Mr. Redd took the vibrator and activated it. He placed the sex toy on Emily's clitoris and started rubbing it slowly, causing her to shiver with pleasure. Emily moaned from the vibration that tingled her sensitive womanly spot. Then, Mr. Redd inserted the vibrator halfway inside Emily's vaginal opening.

"How does that feel?" he asked.

Emily responded with her moans. "Wonderful," she said.

Mr. Redd grinned. Then, he pulled out the vibrator and walked away. But when he returned, he pulled a thick, leather bullwhip from the closet. He began to whip Emily on the butt hard. "You left the house without permission again, didn't you?" he asked. Emily looked up at him and said nothing. Mr. Redd whipped her again with even more brutal hits. "I'm waiting, Emily," he said. "Answer the fucking question!" Emily's eyes filled with tears from the stinging pain.

"Yes, Sir," she replied. "I did leave the house again."

Mr. Redd's eyes turned crimson as he beat Emily vigorously with the bullwhip in his playroom. He knew that Emily was lying to him. "You thought you could lie to the devil?" he said. "Well, think again. I know when you are lying to me by the smell of your body."

Emily was shocked to realize that Mr. Redd knew about her leaving the house and getting caught in the rain afterward.

"So much for keeping this a secret," she thought. Mr. Redd continued to whip her harder, leaving multiple scars on her body.

"Who went to a church and tried to pray to God," he said. "He can't save you like the police and the judge. No one can save you." When he finished, he began to penetrate Emily from behind. He gripped Emily's hips with his claws and forcefully thrust his massive cock inside Emily's butt. Emily was in excruciating pain from Mr. Redd's dominating penetration in the playroom. "I don't like being annoyed," Mr. Redd growled. "So don't FUCKING piss me off!" He continued pounding Emily faster and harder until he released his orgasm inside her. He uncuffed her ankles and wrists from the spreader bar.

Emily stood before him, wholly bruised and overwhelmed by the pain inflicted upon her by Mr. Redd. "Why do you hate God?" she asked.

Mr. Redd choked Emily hard for mentioning God in his presence. "I told you not to mention his name," he roared. "If you think he exists, why don't you pray for him?"

Mr. Redd smacked Emily randomly to make her pray to see if there was a God to save her. But there wasn't. "There is no God," he said. "He does not exist." Emily burst into tears after getting slapped and spanked by Mr. Redd. But it only made him furious. He picked her up and chained her to the X-cross on the wall with leather cuffs. "Since you wanna act like a brat," said Mr. Redd. "You will be treated like a brat!" After he finished, Mr. Redd left the playroom and locked Emily inside alone as punishment to think about what she had done. Emily struggled from her restraints on the X-cross as she watched Mr. Redd close the door behind her.

Over the next few weeks, Mr. Redd treated Emily like a servant in his penthouse to teach her a lesson about obedience. Emily had to clean the place daily, do the laundry, and vacuum the living room while Mr. Redd went to work. He would watch Emily clean his penthouse daily while wearing a French maid outfit. Every night, whenever he came home, he would take Emily to his playroom and perform his BDSM sex on her. Afterward, he would keep her there until she learned to respect him as her master. Mr. Redd made Emily do everything he demanded, including joining him in his playroom for nights of BDSM sex, going out to clubs in the red-light district, and wearing provocative lingerie outfits for him.

He even made Emily have sex with him in public. It made Emily feel sick. She wasn't getting any pleasure at all from him. But he was the kind of man who did not take "No" for an answer. Mr. Redd would punish her and lock her in his playroom if she did. Her non-romantic, sexual relationship with Mr. Redd had left her overwhelmed with fear and anger. She was still aching all over her body from all the nights of BDSM sex she had had with him. Emily didn't want to be treated like a prisoner anymore.

# Chapter 12

Two months later, in the following November, Emily felt weak and miserable. She awoke and got out of bed. She saw her reflection in the mirror. Her body was covered in scars, her skin was pale and bruised, her eyes were red from her constant crying, her throat was dry as sandpaper, and her hair was a tangled mess. She had very little physical strength.

As she entered the living room, Emily joined Mr. Redd for breakfast. She'd had trouble sleeping the previous night after what happened in the playroom. The stinging pain in her butt was so sore that it was hard for her to sit down. Mr. Redd knew that the pain he inflicted on her was to teach her a lesson about respecting her master. "Be glad you live with me," said Mr. Redd. "Most women end up on the street after leaving me. You're lucky I haven't sent you to hell for lying. You'd be dead now if I did."

Emily looked at Mr. Redd with disgust. She didn't want to join him for breakfast. "You've condemned me to hell," she said.

But Mr. Redd was the dominant one, and she couldn't refuse him. "Not yet, I've condemned you," he said. "Don't forget, I am the dominant." So she ate breakfast with him in the dining room without saying a word.

They later left the penthouse and went to Redd Enterprises, Inc. Emily felt pale and tired. Her scars were visible to every employee in the office. Mr. Redd ordered his employees to return to work without questioning him. He was indeed commanding and controlling. Emily felt fear of being near him. He was a monster. Throughout the day, Emily remained with Mr. Redd as his submissive at work. She didn't give him conflict or question him all day. However, it made Emily feel ashamed. When Mr. Redd noticed how miserable Emily was feeling, he began to kiss her on her lips. His tongue slid into her mouth as his hands wrapped around her. Emily tried to break free from his kiss, but her body wasn't responding. Mr. Redd had taken complete control of Emily's body. He pulled away from her lips and grabbed her throat. "Has my seed taken over your mind?" he asked.

Emily felt dizzy from his kiss. She was losing focus. Her resistance was failing. She couldn't protest against his dominance. Mr. Redd has entirely owned Emily's body and soul. He kissed her again and again until Emily surrendered to submission to the point where she fainted in Mr. Redd's arms. Emily was so unconscious that it startled the workers. "Does she need a doctor?" one of the assistants asked.

Mr. Redd informed his assistants to return to work. "I'll take care of her," he said. He left the office with Emily in his arms and took her out of the building.

Later, Mr. Redd brought Emily to his limo. Mr. Redd got in with her and closed the door. "Luxuria Apartment," he told the chauffeur. The Chauffeur drove off down the road from Redd Enterprises, Inc., back to Mr. Redd's penthouse. Mr. Redd brought

Emily to the living room. He set her down on the leather couch and woke her.

Emily awakened and looked up at Mr. Redd. "Where am I?" she said. "What happened?"

Mr. Redd sat down next to her and placed his hand on her breast. "You passed out in my office," he said. "But don't worry. I made sure you were safe." He leaned over to kiss Emily again. But Emily remembered what happened. Mr. Redd made her faint just by kissing her.

She got up from the couch in protest. "You did this to me," she said. Mr. Redd didn't like how Emily acted towards him. He got up from the couch and walked up to her.

"What did I say about pissing me off?" he said.

Emily shook her head. "You *ARE* a Monster," she yelled. "You promised me a life of luxury, and you turned me into a prisoner! You labeled me as a "whore" and now everyone hates me!"

Mr. Redd forcefully threw Emily onto the couch. "I don't like your tone," he said. It made Emily furious at how he was treating her.

"My parents were right about you," she said. Mr. Redd was getting annoyed with Emily's mention of her parents.

"Will you shut up about your goddamn parents?" he shouted. "They're not here. Deal with it. I told you to forget about your parents! They mean nothing to you!"

Emily panicked at realizing Mr. Redd's dominating and intimidating behavior towards her. "They kept you as an 'Ugly Duckling,' and I made you a Swan," he said. "But if you wanna continue to act like a brat, you will be punished if you don't behave!"

Emily gasped. She didn't want him to treat her like a brat. "You can't do this to me," she said. "What about my family? What about my home in Halo Town? What about my life?"

Mr. Redd grew angry at her and snapped. "THIS IS YOUR LIFE!!" he shouted. "Unless you want your life destroyed and you end up in HELL, YOU WILL STAY HERE WITH ME AND DO AS I SAY!!"

Emily burst into tears from Mr. Redd's fury. "You can't control me like this," she said. "You can't!"

Mr. Redd growled at Emily for standing up to him. "Oh yes, I can," he said. As before, Mr. Redd brought Emily to his playroom and put her on the x-cross. Emily's eyes began to fill with tears. But it only made Mr. Redd angry to see a woman cry in the presence of a man. His hand wrapped around her neck, and he began to choke her slightly. "I don't need any tears from you," he growled. "If you don't stop crying, I'll have to spank you again." Emily tried to hold back her tears to avoid getting another spanking. Mr. Redd was pleased.

Then, he began to have sex with her again. Emily was feeling tired, and her wrists hurt so much from the bondage. But Mr. Redd didn't listen to her. He thrusted his hips into her. "Still think this is like Fifty Shades of Grey?" Mr. Redd asked.

Emily looked into his eyes with resentment. Mr. Redd choked Emily's neck harder. "Well, that means you are Fifty shades of fucked up," he growled.

Emily turned her eyes away from him and began to cry. Mr. Redd forcefully began to penetrate her into submission on the X-cross. His long nails dug into her flesh, leaving blood marks in various places. Emily cried in pain from the scratches he was leaving her with. "Don't fight me, Emily," Mr. Redd grunted. "No one can save you now!"

When Mr. Redd finished, he uncuffed her from her bonds, released Emily from the X-cross, and took her out of the playroom. They entered the living room, and Emily looked out the penthouse's window. The city below glowed dimly in the distance. From the top of a skyscraper, a pale blue beacon shone. Emily had seen too much red for one lifetime. She no longer wanted to be with Mr. Redd. Emily felt like Eve from the story about a woman who had tasted the forbidden fruit and was cast out of the garden forever. She forgot about her home in Halo Town and her family as she closed the curtains. Mr. Redd pulled Emily away from the window and brought her into his bedroom.

Emily got into bed, and Mr. Redd gave her a glass of wine to drink. "I'm not thirsty," she said. Mr. Redd frowned at Emily, who rejected his offer. He slapped Emily in the face and forced her to drink.

"Drink the fucking wine," he growled. Emily still didn't want the wine. Mr. Redd had to make Emily drink it against her will. He grabbed her head and poured the wine into her mouth. Emily choked a little from the forced consumption she endured. The wine had a bitter and sour taste. Emily coughed afterward. Mr. Redd looked at Emily, growling. "Now you know how it feels to be treated like a brat who misbehaves," he said, his tone bitter. "You have no one to blame but yourself." Emily looked down at the floor as more tears fell from her eyes.

In the middle of the night, Emily was asleep in Mr. Redd's bed. While she was sleeping, she began to have a dream. But her dream turned into a nightmare. In her dream, she was chained to a bed, completely naked. The room was lit in red, surrounded by candles on black candle holders. The room was Mr. Redd's bedroom. There was a mirror above the bed, which showed Emily's reflection. Suddenly, she heard a voice coming from the corner of the room. "You shall give your body to me," the voice said. Out of the shadows was Mr. Redd, dressed in a red robe. As he approached the bed, he repeated the exact words to Emily. Then, Mr. Redd began to ask her a simple question, hoping for an answer. "What would you give me for pleasure?" he said. Emily tried to get free, but the chains began to tighten around her wrists and ankles. Mr. Redd's eyes turned red as he removed his robe before Emily. His body was completely naked and oiled. Emily gasped at the sight of him as he positioned himself on top of her body.

He inserted his cock inside Emily and began to have sex with her. The sounds emerging from his mouth appeared more beastly than human. "Would you give me your body?" Mr. Redd asked. Emily whimpered in pain as Mr. Redd penetrated her brutally into his bed. As the two had sex, Emily looked up at the mirror above the bed. To her horror, she could see Mr. Redd's reflection. But his reflection showed his devil form penetrating her. His skin was red, with a tail and horns on his head. Emily got scared at the sight of Mr. Redd's devil form. Emily struggled to escape because the weight of Mr. Redd's body on top of hers was weighing her down in the bed.

Mr. Redd looked into Emily's eyes and gave her a sinister grin. "Would you give me your soul?" Mr. Redd asked. His voice almost sounded like a demon. Emily could see his eyes turning red like the demon he was. She struggled to escape, but Mr. Redd grabbed her neck tightly with one hand. He didn't want her to escape. "Don't fight me, Emily," he said. "You shall submit to me! You shall give in to my fucking!"

Mr. Redd opened his mouth to reveal a pair of fangs to Emily and let out a roar. Emily let out a scream as Mr. Redd began to bite her on the neck. Emily woke up screaming in bed. Her heart pounded in her chest, and she breathed, sweat rolling down her face. Emily was still alive, but her nightmare felt real, as if it was telling her something terrible was going to happen to her. "What a nightmare," she said. She could still feel her heart beating inside her chest.

The next morning, Emily woke up from a brutal night with her body covered in scars from the whips Mr. Redd gave her. She could see that the room was empty. Mr. Redd had gone to work, leaving Emily alone in his penthouse. Emily quietly got out of bed and got dressed. A few minutes later, Emily left Mr. Redd's bedroom and headed to the elevator. As she left the building, Emily wandered through the city alone. Her body was sore and aching in pain. Her eyes were red with sadness from constant crying.

Suddenly, the sky above her turned dark and gray, as if it were about to rain. It was the same weather she saw back in Halo Town. Everyone gave her a dirty look as they passed by, calling her names because she was in a relationship with Mr. Redd. Emily was named "Satan's Whore" by every person in Diablo City. The glamour faded into a dark gray ambiance around her. The neon signs became dreary and cold, and the Devil's Playground became filthy and dirty, littered with empty, broken bottles and tattered posters. Thunder shook the sky as Emily entered a nearby park, where she went to clear her mind. She sat on a bench and sighed. Emily looked up and watched couples strolling hand in hand. Emily was feeling completely miserable. "Mom and Dad were right," she thought. "I shouldn't date a man who is a sadist."

Just then, an older man walked up and sat on the bench beside her. He was a black preacher from a church. He wore a white robe and a black suit underneath. He looked at Emily, who was crying.

"What's wrong, my child?" he asked.

Emily looked up at him and dried her face. "Who are you?" she asked.

"Just call me a friend," the black preacher said. "I can't help but notice you sitting here alone. What seems to be the problem?"

Emily began to tell the black preacher the truth. "I sold my soul to the devil for a life of luxury," she explained.

The black preacher scratched his chin. "So you sold your soul to the devil?" he said.

"Yes," Emily answered. "His name is Mr. Redd. He's a multi-billionaire and the owner of Redd Enterprises Inc."

The black preacher asked her how it happened.

Emily told him about her life experience when she met Mr. Redd. "I met him a few days ago in Halo Town," she said. "He said I was beautiful and treated me like a princess. He invited me to dinner at a restaurant called La Flamme Rouge, and then he took me to his penthouse apartment, where he had sex with me."

The black preacher was shocked to hear her say those words in a church. But he told her to continue. "Mr. Redd wined and dined me and showered me with presents," Emily said. "Then, he made me his prisoner. Mr. Redd took me to his BDSM playroom and had sex with me. I told him I didn't want to be his submissive, but he threatened me with submitting to him. Mr. Redd spanked me and whipped me with floggers and crop whips. He's like a devil version of Christian Grey, only darker. He feeds on the pain and suffering of others like a Demon. A BDSM Demon. He posted a video of me having sex with him on the internet, which got me expelled from Halo University." Emily began to cry as she continued telling him the rest of her story. "I lost my parents, who saw the video on their computer," she said. "They moved out of my house and said they no longer needed me because I had disgraced them."

The black preacher sat beside her, telling her she should dismiss his deal. But Emily couldn't, not after what Mr. Redd did to her. "I can't escape from him," she said. "He'll look for me and bring me back to his penthouse to punish me. He's a sadistic monster. He's never going to let me go. He'll keep torturing me until I'm dead. No one will mourn for me."

The black preacher calmed her down gently. "Only you make the decisions," he said. "It's your life. Be grateful for the life you have." But Emily was not grateful. She felt ashamed and heartbroken simultaneously. The man she had fallen in love with was a sadist and a devil. He only wanted her soul.

"What should I do?" she said in tears.

The black preacher placed his hand on her shoulder. "Everyone makes mistakes," he said. "We learn from them as we navigate life.

You know you made a mistake. Now, you must learn from it. Sometimes, the things we want are not the things we need. Learn to let go of temptation."

Emily trembled, tears welling up in her eyes. "But what about my soul?" she said. "Mr. Redd owns me, and I can't escape him. I feel like he's controlling me through my soul."

The black preacher explained to her that her soul was special and who her soul belonged to.

"Your soul doesn't belong to Mr. Redd," he said. "It belongs to God. He created every soul on Earth. We are born into this world with a choice we make daily. We learn to let go of our past and move forward. The best way is to learn to forgive yourself. Look inside your heart and pray to God for forgiveness."

Emily dried her tears as she looked up at the sky. "Learn to forgive myself," she thought. "I was swept up in the glamour of luxury that I had forgotten who I was long ago." The black preacher placed his hand on Emily's shoulder. "Have faith in yourself and God," he said. "I hope you will feel better."

The black preacher got up from the bench and returned to the church to attend to his duties. He turned to look at Emily and smiled. "I'm glad we had this talk," he said. Emily waved "goodbye" to him as she got up from the bench and left the park. She began to think about what the preacher had said to her in the park about making choices and having hope.

Suddenly, Emily saw Mr. Redd standing before her. He was furious. "How did you find me?" she asked.

Mr. Redd growled at Emily for leaving his penthouse for the fourth time. "All I needed to find you was to follow your heartbeat," he said. Emily was frightened to see him. Mr. Redd approached her with red eyes. "If you're thinking about talking to God, you can just forget it," he says. "He can't save you. I am the only one who cares for you. I am your only friend. And you will stay with me forever."

In fear, Emily backed away, but it only made him angrier. "Stay back," she said. "Don't come any closer! I mean it! NO! Don't!!"

Mr. Redd picked up Emily and took her to his car. "I believe you will find that resistance is futile," he said. "You're coming home with me. No escaping this time." Then, he drove her back to his penthouse in rage.

As they returned, Mr. Redd threw Emily to the floor. His appearance startled Emily. He gave her a menacing stare. "I am *VERY* disappointed in you, Emily," he shouted. "You disobeyed me! Now I'm going to have to punish you!"

Emily stood and stepped away in fear. "I thought you'd be at work," Emily said.

Mr. Redd frowned. "I told you I am incapable of leaving you alone," he said. "Now, why did you leave my penthouse?"

Emily explained that she needed to get away from him. "You're too dominant and controlling," she said. "I had to leave so I could get away. Away from you!"

Mr. Redd grew angry. "I said you will never leave me," he said. "Do I need to remind you again?"

Emily didn't want Mr. Redd to remind her of his dominance over her. She just needed to get away from him. "Don't you think I've had enough of this already?" she said.

"There's no such thing as having enough," Mr. Redd said. "This is how I treat all my assistants. You should know that already because that's how you will be treated from now on if you pull a stunt like that again!!"

Mr. Redd brought Emily to his playroom and beat her with his belt. All that Mr. Redd heard from her was the sound of painful tears coming from her eyes.

Then, he slapped her multiple times in the face. "Where is your God now?"

Emily didn't answer him. Mr. Redd furiously waited for Emily's reply. So he beat her again.

"There is no God," Emily whimpered. Mr. Redd didn't hear her. He smacked her again to make her say her answer.

"I want to fucking hear it," he growled. "Is there a God?"

Emily answered his question again with tears in her eyes. "There is no God," she said.

Mr. Redd smirked. "That's right," he said. "Don't you forget it next time! If you leave my penthouse again, you will go straight to Hell!"

Mr. Redd threw Emily against the wall. He secured her wrists and ankles on the x-cross, leaving blisters on her skin. "You broke the rules," he growled. "And for that, you will rot in this playroom!" Mr. Redd left Emily in his playroom and headed to work in his limo.

Later that evening, Emily stopped crying. But she still felt sore from the pain Mr. Redd had inflicted on her earlier that day. Mr. Redd opened the door and saw Emily still on the x-cross. He removed her from her bonds and brought her into his bedroom. He lay her down on his bed and removed her clothes until she was completely naked. Emily still felt hurt both physically and emotionally. She lay in bed with tears in her eyes. Mr. Redd saw Emily's body covered in scars. He walked up to her and towered over her.

"I hope you learned your lesson, my dear," he said. Emily looked up at him and frowned. "You must know that when I tell you there is no God, I mean there is no God," said Mr. Redd. "You must never again mention his name or even pray to him. He does not exist." Emily's eyes watered from listening to Mr. Redd's explanation. "You must also know that you are never to escape from me," Mr. Redd continued. "You are under contract because if you try to escape from me again, I will destroy you." Emily had heard enough. She turned away from him because she didn't want him to see her cry.

"Why do you treat me like a prisoner?" she asked.

Mr. Redd brought Emily's face to him and answered her question. "You left my penthouse for the fourth time," he said. "I specifically told you never to leave me. Now you know the penalty for disobeying me: I'll send you to Hell if you leave me again."

Emily didn't want to stay with Mr. Redd.

"It's your choice, Emily," Mr. Redd said. "Either you stay with me forever or burn in hell? Which is it?"

Emily didn't have an answer. She was too tired. Mr. Redd let go of her face and left the bedroom. "I'll give you time to think about it," he said. "I expect an answer when I come back. So don't go anywhere." Emily said nothing, and Mr. Redd closed the door and went into his office to do some work.

When Emily woke up, she quietly left Mr. Redd's bedroom and slept in the guest bedroom. She didn't want another argument with him. As she slept, she heard a voice coming from nowhere. Emily got out of bed to see who the voice was. Then, she came upon a mirror and looked into her reflection. A glow of white light appeared around it as if an angel had appeared before her.

"Emily," said her reflection.

Emily asked, "Who are you?"

Her reflection replied, "I am your conscience."

Emily was surprised to see her conscience in the mirror. It was strange to talk to her reflection in the middle of the night. "What are you doing here?" Emily asked.

"I am here to show you who you once were before you met the Devil," said her conscience.

A soft glow revealed Emily's past life in the mirror. Emily saw herself as a remarkable young woman with a loving family, enjoying a vibrant and fulfilling life while embracing independence and freedom. Even from her mistakes, she had learned.

When the image faded, her conscience reappeared. "You can still right the wrong," said her conscience. "There is still a chance to change your ways."

Emily felt a warm glow inside her. A beam of light shone on her face, illuminating the glow of her realization. She could still end her relationship with Mr. Redd. There was still hope inside her heart.

"I know what I must do," she said to herself.

"Yes," said her conscience. "Correct your mistake."

Emily's conscience disappeared, only to return to her reflection in the mirror. Emily knew she must end her relationship with Mr. Redd tomorrow morning.

# Chapter 13

The following day, Emily woke up and got dressed. She felt a little better after getting a good night's rest. Emily looked at herself in the mirror and remembered what her conscience had told her. Then, she began confronting Mr. Redd face-to-face. She had to be the one to break her deal with him alone, even if he didn't take "No" for an answer. Emily wanted out of their relationship forever. At first, Emily shook nervously but remembered what the preacher had said. After deep breathing, Emily cleared her mind and left the guest's bedroom. She found Mr. Redd talking with a client in the living room. Emily walked up to him firmly. Mr. Redd looked at Emily and smiled.

"Good morning," he said. "So nice to see you awake. Have you decided to stay with me?"

Emily said nothing to him. She had not decided to stay with Mr. Redd.

Then, he offered Emily a glass of wine from his cabinet. But Emily declined his offer. She was not happy to see Mr. Redd. Emily wanted to discuss with him about their sexual relationship and how difficult it had been for her. But then, Mr. Redd noticed Emily was not wearing her black mini-dress.

"Why aren't you wearing your black dress?" he asked.

Emily shook her head and frowned. "I took it off," she said. "I'm not a toy for you to play with."

Mr. Redd showed Emily the contract. "May I remind you of the contract?" he said. "You need a little discipline to teach you a lesson."

But Emily interrupted him. She cleared her throat to make her statement as straightforward as possible. "I don't want to be your prisoner," she said. "I've been living with you for three months, and it's time to say enough. I want my old life back as it used to be."

Mr. Redd was stunned. "What do you mean?" he asked.

Emily explained to him that she no longer wanted to continue their relationship. "I want to cancel our contract, Mr. Redd," she added. "I'm done being your sex slave."

But Mr. Redd didn't care. "Let me remind you, Emily," he said. "I own you! That's why you signed the contract! Once you belong to me, you can *NEVER* go back!"

Emily said, "No."

Mr. Redd frowns.

"This is not what I wanted. It's not what I wished for."

Mr. Redd raised an eyebrow. "Are you saying you don't want me anymore?" he said.

"Yes," Emily replied. "Our relationship is not going to work out for us. You lied to me and treated me like a prisoner in your own house. You gave me nothing but pain and suffering."

Mr. Redd thought she was kidding. He tried to approach her and kiss her, but Emily stepped back in disgust. "Don't come any closer!" she said.

Mr. Redd frowned at her dismissal. "Why won't you let me kiss you?" Mr. Redd asked.

Emily told him she didn't want to be treated like a servant in his household. She explained why she wanted a life of luxury before meeting him. "All my life, I wished to be popular," said Emily. "To be accepted by others instead of being treated like an outcast. I thought if someone could wave a magic wand and make that happen, I'd have a happy ending. But I realize that it doesn't work that way. Life is not a fairy tale. It's a reality. I've seen the consequences of my wish for luxury and its price. That's why I want to end our relationship to regain my old life."

Mr. Redd was annoyed with Emily's words. He was so annoyed that he smashed the bottle of wine on his desk. He slowly walked to the couch and lowered his head like he was about to cry.

"You want to end our relationship and go home to your family," he said. Emily noticed how upset Mr. Redd was. His hands gripped the head of the couch; from his mouth, the sound of growling and his fists clenched in hatred. However, she didn't want to approach him. "You would rather be with the family that never loved you than be with me," Mr. Redd added. "That's your decision?"

Emily nodded in response. "I love my family," she said. "And I need them more than luxury itself. They're more important to me."

Mr. Redd clenched his fists, hearing Emily's words about her family. "So it's okay to let me go?" Emily asked.

Mr. Redd turns to her with anger because he didn't want to experience another heartbreak. "NO," he said in a stern tone. "It's NOT okay. A deal's a deal. You get a life of luxury and sex, and I get your soul. Now stop talking, and let me fuck you."

Emily frowned at him.

"I won't let you do it," she said. Mr. Redd arched his eyebrow at Emily.

"Before you get all high and mighty with me, I think I should warn you," he said. Now, Mr. Redd was getting angry at her. He slowly transformed into his devil form in front of her to intimidate her into surrendering to him. But Emily didn't feel scared for a minute. It only made Mr. Redd's fury grow more and more. "I'm not all glamour and charm," he said. "I **DO** have a dark side, and believe me, it's not charming. Now, you can go easy or go hard. But one way or another, I *will* destroy you!" But Emily still refused. She was serious. Emily didn't want to lose what was left of her life to him.

"I WON'T LET YOU," she said. "And there's nothing you can say or do to change my mind."

Now burning with fury and wrath, Mr. Redd growled at Emily. "Oh, I think you'll change your mind," he growled. "Because you leave **NO CHOICE!**"

Mr. Redd picked Emily up over his shoulder and brought her to the playroom to punish her severely. He threw her onto the bed and bound her hands and feet with leather cuffs. "Let me go," Emily shouted. Mr. Redd didn't want to let her go. He was furious with her.

"You want me to be the monster?" he asked. "Then, so be it!" With a mighty roar, Mr. Redd transformed into a devilish version of himself with burning red eyes and sharp fangs. Emily saw his demon form and screamed in fear. Mr. Redd roared at Emily in anger. He pulled out a flaming bullwhip and gave Emily a harsh whipping on her body to make her change her mind. With force in his arm, he slammed the whip down onto Emily's body, leaving scorching, red-hot marks. Emily cried in pain from the flaming whip as her body was being whipped. Mr. Redd wrapped the whip around Emily's neck like a python snake and straddled her. He pinned her wrists down on the bed to prevent her from escaping.

Mr. Redd's eyes were burning with wrath and fury. "**NOW LISTEN TO ME, YOU LITTLE BITCH,**" he roared in his demon voice. "**THIS IS YOUR LAST CHANCE BEFORE I WHIP YOU TO OBLIVION! STAY WITH ME, OR FOREVER BURN IN HELL!**"

But Emily stopped him by shouting, "No! I want my old life back! I don't want to stay with you!"

Mr. Redd looked at her with anger as he raised his claws. **"THEN, I WILL SEND YOU TO HELL FOREVER!!"** shouted Mr. Redd. Emily knew this was too much for her to take. Mr. Redd was literally about to kill her in his playroom. But Emily remembered that she still had a safe word to use if things became too intense. All she had to do was say it out loud. As Mr. Redd was about to kill her, Emily shouted out, "I WISH FOR **FREEDOM!!"**

Mr. Redd heard her words and stopped whipping her. He saw that Emily had used her safe word at the last minute. Mr. Redd removed himself from Emily and returned to his human form. Then, he put down the whip and freed her, pulling her from her bounds and gently leading her out of the playroom. He locked the door and put his key away. Mr. Redd never opened the door to his playroom again. Then, he went into the living room and sat on the couch. Emily needed clarification. She came up to him on the couch and asked him why he didn't kill her.

"Why didn't you attack me?" she asked.

Mr. Redd explained to Emily that he didn't kill her because she used her safe word. "You used your safeword," he said. "At the last minute, too. I'm surprised you're still alive. The safe word you said was a deal breaker." Emily was confused. She didn't know that her safe word was a deal breaker.

"A deal breaker?" Emily asked. "What do you mean?"

Mr. Redd looked at her and told her about what she did. "Didn't you read the contract?" he said. "Article 1, Section 47, Paragraph 9, Subsection 3: Selfless Acts of Redemption. It says, 'If you commit one truly benevolent act, it voids the contract.' In short, that means you get to keep your soul."

Emily's eyes grew wide with surprise. "I get to keep my soul?" she asked.

Mr. Redd answered, "Yes. You get to keep your soul. I no longer own you. I release you."

Emily's eyes grew wide when she heard that she would be able to keep her soul. "You mean I'm free?" she asked.

Mr. Redd sighed. "Yes, you're free to go," he said.

Emily was thrilled. She got her old life back, and she got to keep her soul. Mr. Redd shook his head in annoyance. He was disappointed with Emily's decision. "I've been doing this for 6,000 years," he said. "And you're the first person to give up a life of selfish luxury. I hope it doesn't appear on the 6 o'clock news."

Emily looked at Mr. Redd. She was curious to know why he acted friendly when he was supposed to be angry at her. "Why are you suddenly so nice to me?" she asked.

Mr. Redd explained the concepts of good and evil to Emily. "God and I exist on Earth," he said. "Good and evil both work in mysterious ways. But it comes down to you, Emily. You don't have to look far for Heaven and Hell. They're right here on Earth. You make the choice. And you've just made yours."

Emily realized this and smiled. "So does this mean I can go home?" she asked.

Mr. Redd looked at her with disappointment. "Yes, you can go home," he said. "I liked you, you know? You're beautiful."

Emily realized that she had found redemption and hugged Mr. Redd. "You have been the kindest gentleman I've ever met," she said. "Even though you can be a little controlling."

Mr. Redd smiled at Emily one last time before letting her go. "Go home," Mr. Redd said at last. "You'll forget about me. After all, I'm the devil. My place is here."

So Emily said goodbye to Mr. Redd and left his penthouse. Mr. Redd said goodbye to Emily afterward.

As Emily left the penthouse, she felt a sense of relief and joy that she was finally free. She got to keep her soul at last. Emily was no longer Mr. Redd's submissive toy; she was free. Emily didn't look back at the penthouse behind her. She got on the next bus back to Halo Town. As the bus drove off, the black preacher from the park watched Emily and smiled. "Well done, Emily," he said. As he walked away, angel wings appeared on his back, then vanished into thin air. Emily looked out the window and waved goodbye to Diablo City, never to return for the rest of her life.

Emily returned home to Halo Town, where she saw her family waiting outside her house. Everything had returned to normal; all the events that happened to her with Mr. Redd were now distant memories. Emily's parents and her older brother, Marcus, had returned to the house, but they were happy to see her this time. Emily was glad to be home again with her family. She missed them so much. "I'm sorry I didn't listen to you," she said. "You were right about Mr. Redd."

But her parents stopped her for a minute. They told her that they were the ones who were sorry. "We've forgotten how much of a woman you've become," Mr. Richards said. "We were wrong about you. You're not a mistake."

Emily understood him and apologized for being ignorant of her parents' warnings. "I admit I made a mistake," she said. "But I've learned from it."

Mrs. Richards approached Emily and embraced her. "You're unique in your way," she said. "You're our daughter, and we love you."

Emily was surprised. For the first time, her family finally accepted her. She smiled and cried tears of joy. "I love you," she said at last. Marcus apologized to her for everything he said and had done to her.

"I didn't mean to make fun of you," he said. Emily forgave him and hugged him.

"You're my brother," she said. "That's all that matters."

She hugged her family, and they all headed inside together. Emily was finally part of the family again. Emily went inside her house with her family and had dinner with them.

One year later, on Tuesday in April, Emily was 20 years old and returned to her ordinary life. Her body no longer had scars all over, her red marks were all gone, and her wrists and buttocks were no longer blistered. Emily felt like a new woman. She learned her lesson in her life. Emily learned to have hope and faith, be grateful for her life, and be happy. She woke up one morning and got out of bed feeling like a fresh field of grass that had grown in the Spring. She got dressed in the new clothes that her parents finally bought for her instead of her old, hand-me-down clothes. As Emily came downstairs, she said "Good morning" to Mr. and Mrs. Richards in the living room. Marcus was a little nicer to Emily instead of making fun of her. Emily sat down at the table for breakfast. Mrs. Richards told Emily she received a call from Dean Woodrow at Halo University. "You're going back to college," she said. "Dean Woodrow wanted to give you a second chance." Emily was happy to be going back to college again. She got a second chance. Emily finished her breakfast and began to leave the house.

"I'll see you later," she said.

Emily arrived at Halo University just as before, but with a change. She wasn't late. The students were no longer teasing her or calling her names. Emily felt so alive now that things were back to normal. She was attending college, doing well in class, and paying attention. Emily headed inside the building with a new sense of purpose. As she approached class, she saw Nicole, Katie, and Jetta approach her. Nicole was still bitter at Emily for dating Mr. Redd.

"Hey, Richards," she said sarcastically. "How did your date go with the Redd Man? Did he take advantage of you in any way? Or maybe he didn't want to date you because you're an ugly, dirty duckling. No one will ever love you."

Emily stood up for herself and confronted Nicole, but she didn't want to harm her. So she let her go.

"Nice talking with you, Nicole," she said. Emily headed to class feeling like her true self. Nicole was left speechless, especially Jetta and Katie.

"Looks like Emily has found her confidence," said Jetta. Nicole frowned. She didn't like how confident Emily was feeling today. Nicole was still angry with her because Emily had become widespread.

"I *HATE* Emily Richards," she hissed. "I'd sell my soul to the devil to destroy that Richards bitch once and for all!"

Just then, Mr. Redd appeared dressed as a college teacher and stood before Nicole. "I can arrange it," he said in a seductive tone.

Nicole looked at him oddly. He presented the college girls with a contract and a red pen for them to use. "All you have to do is sign your name on this contract," he said. "And I will make your wish come true."

However, Nicole declined his offer and shrugged him off. "Changed my mind," she said. She walked away without looking back at him. Jetta and Katie followed behind her as they headed to class together. Mr. Redd was left disappointed as he watched the three ladies leave him.

"So be it, then," he said. "You won't be seeing me anymore." Devastated, he left the college campus and returned to Diablo City in his limo. He was never seen or heard from again.

Later that day, Emily headed downtown to look at new window displays. Walking down the street, she bumped into a man running in the opposite direction. **"BOOM!"** She helped the man to his feet. "Are you okay?" The man, 20 years old with blonde hair, introduced himself as Donald McKane. He looked just like Emily, the only difference being that he wore glasses. He looked up at her and was amazed.

"Hello," he said.

Emily smiled and said, "Hello." She asked him for his name.

"My name is Donald McKane," he replied.

"I'm Emily Richards," she said. The two smiled at each other. Then, she picked up his books and papers. "Would you like to join me for a smoothie?" Emily asked.

"Yes," Donald replied. "We can go to an art exhibit downtown afterward."

Emily agreed, and she and Donald headed to a café downtown for smoothies. Emily was happy to be accepted for who she was, just by being herself. She was also excited to be in a relationship that made her feel comfortable and with the right guy. She never thought of Mr. Redd again. She had forgotten about him and would never sell her soul to him for a life of luxury. Her soul was more important than luxury itself.

Ultimately, Emily Richards could never ask for a better life than this. She was happy and grateful for her life, having already achieved what she needed—a happy life in Halo Town.

# The End

*"Be grateful for the life you have."*

**-Jasminne Aurora McDonald**

48978CB00011BA/441